THE RESTRAINT OF BEASTS

MAGNUS MILLS failed his 11-Plus in 1965 and was then placed in the hands of Gloucestershire Education Authority. He later worked with dangerous machinery in Britain and Australia, before obtaining his present employment as a London bus driver.

THE RESTRAINT
OF BEASTS

MAGNUS MILLS

Flamingo
An Imprint of HarperCollins*Publishers*

Flamingo
An Imprint of HarperCollins*Publishers*
77–85 Fulham Palace Road,
Hammersmith, London W6 8JB

Published by Flamingo 1998
3 5 7 9 8 6 4 2

A catalogue record for this book is
available from the British Library

ISBN 0 00 225720 3

Set in Postscript Linotype Meridien by
Rowland Phototypesetting Ltd,
Bury St Edmunds, Suffolk

Printed and bound in Great Britain by
Clays Ltd, St Ives plc

FOR SUE

1

'I'm putting you in charge of Tam and Richie,' said Donald. 'They can't go to England on their own.'

'No, I suppose not.'

'We'd never know what they were getting up to.'

'No.'

'So you can take over as foreman from today.'

'Right.'

He allowed me a few moments to absorb the news, then asked, 'Are you finding it hot in here?'

'Just a little, yes,' I replied.

'You should have said.' Donald rose from behind his desk and moved to the skirting board, where a radiator pipe emerged. He turned a stop-tap several times, clockwise, before settling again in his chair.

'These things can be controlled,' he remarked. 'Now, are there any questions?'

He sat back and waited. I knew the sort of questions Donald expected me to ask, but I couldn't think of any. Not with him examining me from behind his desk the way he did. At the moment only one obvious question came to mind.

'Why me?'

'There's no one else available. You're the last one.'

'Oh . . . right.'

Donald's gaze remained fixed on me.

'You don't seem very excited about all this,' he said.

'No, no,' I replied. 'Really, I am.'

'Doesn't sound like it. After all, it's not often we appoint a new foreman.'

'No, I know,' I said. 'I just wondered . . . have you told them?'

'Robert has told them.'

'Robert?'

'Yes.'

'Can't you tell them?'

'Robert is quite capable of telling them.' He reached for his typewriter and slid it across the desk towards him. I watched as he placed a sheet of paper in the roller and began tapping the keys. After a while he looked up and saw that I was still standing there.

'Yes?'

'Wouldn't it be better coming from you?' I asked.

'Why's that?'

'It would give me some authority.'

'Haven't you any authority of your own?'

'Yes, but . . .'

'Well, then.' Donald continued looking at me for a long while. 'It's only for a few weeks,' he said. 'Then you can come back.'

He began attending to his typewriter again, so I went out. Donald's mind was obviously made up, therefore further discussion was pointless. Closing the door behind me I paused briefly and listened. Inside the office an unsteady tapping had started up. The decision was probably being committed to paper at this very moment, so that was that. It would have been better if Donald had told them himself, but I really wasn't bothered either way. There was no big deal about the new arrangement. No particular cause for concern. After all, there were only two of them. Should be a piece of cake. True, they had their own way of doing certain things, but that was fair enough. Only to be expected considering how long they'd been together. We'd just have to get used to each other, that's all. I decided to go and see them straight away.

Their pick-up truck was parked at the other side of the yard. They'd been sitting in the cab earlier when I went past on my way to Donald's office. Now, however, there was no sign of them. I walked over and glanced at the jumble of tools and equipment lying in the back of the vehicle. Everything looked as though it had been thrown in there in a great hurry. Clearly it would all need sorting out before we could do anything, so I got in the truck and reversed round to the store room. Then I sat and waited for them to appear. Looking around the inside of the cab I noticed the words 'Tam' and 'Rich' scratched on the dashboard. A plastic lunch box and a bottle of Irn-Bru lay on the shelf.

So where were they? They seemed to have disappeared without trace. From what I'd heard this was the sort of thing they did all the time. They'd just go off somewhere for no apparent reason. And when they came back they wouldn't have an excuse or anything. That's what I'd heard anyway.

Eventually I got fed up with waiting and went round to the timber yard. They were nowhere to be seen, so I then conducted a search of all the store rooms and outhouses. Nothing.

Finally, when I couldn't think of anywhere else to look, I

went back to where I'd started and found them sitting in the truck eating sandwiches. They sat side by side in the double passenger seat, watching me as I approached. I knew Richie by sight. He was the one by the window. Therefore the other one must be Tam.

I spoke through the opening. 'Alright?'

'Alright,' said Richie.

'Just got back?'

'Last night.'

'Looks like we'll need a bit of a sort out,' I said, indicating the gear in the back of the truck. 'But finish your sandwiches first.'

I walked round and got in the cab at the driver's side. Tam looked at me for a moment as I slammed the door shut, but remained silent. I could now see that Richie was providing the sandwiches from the plastic lunch box, perched on his lap. He swigged the Irn-Bru and handed it to Tam.

'Don't leave any floaters in it,' he said.

Tam drank, lowered the bottle, and examined the contents. Then he turned to me. 'Like some?'

'Oh. Thanks.' I took the bottle and drank the warm dregs in the bottom. 'Thanks,' I repeated, handing it back.

'That's OK.' Tam passed the empty bottle back to Richie, who screwed the top back on before throwing it out of the window.

And so we sat there in silence. Richie on one side, Tam in the middle and me behind the steering wheel. All staring through the windscreen. It was a bleak sort of day, with occasional gusts of wind gently rocking the vehicle from side to side.

There was a movement in the distance and Robert came into sight. We watched as he opened a gate to let Ralph through. He appeared to be about to set off on one of his long walks. Whether or not he noticed us sitting there in the truck, watching him, was hard to tell. If he did, he didn't show it. He merely closed the gate behind him and ambled away over the fields.

'Look at Robert,' said Richie. That was all he said, but I could tell by the stifled silence which followed the remark that Tam and Richie were obviously sharing some private joke made at Robert's expense. I didn't join in.

After a short interval I said, 'Did Robert come and speak to you?'

'Just now,' replied Richie.

'Oh. Right. Is that OK with you then?'

'Have to be, won't it?'

'Suppose so,' I said.

Tam glanced at me briefly, but didn't seem to have anything to say on the subject. Instead he turned to Richie. 'Got a fag, Rich?'

Richie reached to a lump I'd noticed in his shirt pocket and took out a cigarette pack. Then he squirmed sideways and fished a lighter from his jeans. He handed Tam a cigarette, gave him a light, lit his own, and we sat there in silence for another few minutes while they smoked, and desultory flecks of rain landed on the cab roof.

'Right,' I said when they'd finished. 'We'd better have a go at sorting out all the gear.' We got out and stood looking into the back of the truck. The collection of tools lay in a shallow pool of rainwater, some of them bent, most of them showing the first signs of rust. This was supposed to be a set of professional fence-building equipment, but actually looked like a hoard of junk. There were hole-digging implements, wire-tightening gear, a rusty steel spike (blunt), a selection of chisels and a chain winch. All in various states of disrepair. Also several coils of wire. The only item that appeared to be in reasonable condition was a large post-hammer with a cast iron head, lying slightly to one side.

'Here's Donald,' murmured Tam, and they both immediately began sorting through the pile. Donald had emerged from his office and was advancing across the yard in our direction. His sudden appearance had a marked effect on Tam and Richie, whose faces showed that they were concentrating hard on their work. Tam leaned over the side of the truck and pulled out the post-hammer.

'Glad to see it's still in one piece,' said Donald as he joined us. He took the hammer from Tam and stood it, head downwards, on the concrete. Richie, meanwhile, had lifted one of the coils of wire onto his shoulder and was about to take it into the store room.

'You seem to be in a great hurry all of a sudden,' said Donald.

This caused Richie to hesitate awkwardly in mid-step with the coil balanced on his shoulder. He half-turned and looked at Tam. Donald was now peering into the back of the truck.

'You people really should take more care of your equipment,' he said.

After a dutiful pause Richie made another move towards the store room but was again brought to a halt by Donald.

'Leave that for now. I've just had a serious phone call. You'd better come into the office.' Without further comment he turned and walked off towards the open door. We all glanced at each other, saying nothing, and filed after him.

On entering the office I saw that Donald had placed two hard chairs side by side facing his desk. I'd seen these hard chairs before. They were slightly less than full adult size, made from wood, and spent most of the time stacked one on top of the other in the corner beside the filing cabinet. That was where they'd been earlier when I was talking to Donald. I'd hardly noticed them really. They just looked as though they were intended to remain there indefinitely. It never occurred to me that these two hard chairs were kept for a particular purpose. They had been positioned squarely and symmetrically in front of the desk, and Tam and Richie did not have to be told where to sit.

I went and stood by the small recessed window, half-leaning against the radiator, which I noticed had been turned up full again. There was one other change. Donald had removed the light-shade from the ceiling and replaced the usual hundred-watt bulb with a more powerful one. This bathed every corner of the office in sharp light.

Slowly and deliberately he settled in his chair and sat for a few moments regarding Tam and Richie across the desk.

'Mr McCrindle's fence has gone slack,' he announced at last.

2

Donald let the words sink in. 'He's just been on the phone. He's very disappointed. You'll have to go back today and put it right. I thought you knew what you were doing.'

He paused. Tam and Richie said nothing.

'I thought you knew what you were doing. You're supposed to be specialists. Mr McCrindle wanted a high-tensile fence, not something to play a game of tennis over. How are you going to progress with future projects if this kind of thing is going to happen all the time? You only finished off Mr McCrindle yesterday.'

I noticed that Tam and Richie looked quite meek while they were being addressed by Donald. They sat in their two hard chairs, which were a little too small for them, avoiding his gaze and staring with interest at his typewriter, or maybe the pencil lying next to it.

'It means you won't be able to go to England until the middle of next week,' Donald continued. 'Convenient for you, isn't it?'

I wasn't sure what he meant by this remark.

'Sorry,' mumbled Tam at last.

Richie mumbled 'Sorry' too.

There was more. 'I've just had a look in the file. It seems you didn't measure the fence.'

Tam looked up briefly. 'Oh,' he said. 'No.'

'How am I supposed to invoice Mr McCrindle if you failed to take a measurement?'

'Don't know.' Tam shuffled his feet slightly. The radiator pipe under the office floor was slowly warming up his rubber boots, so that they stuck momentarily to the lino. Both Tam and Richie were now beginning to look very uncomfortable. Their chairs were so close together that they were pressed against one another, shoulder to shoulder, each in danger of being unbalanced at any moment.

'Why didn't you measure Mr McCrindle's fence?'

'Forgot.'

'Oh, you forgot. It would be a different story if I forgot to pay you, wouldn't it?'

Donald fell silent and sat looking at them, apparently waiting for an answer.

It was Richie who managed to speak this time. 'Suppose so,' he said.

How long Donald kept them sitting there, side by side in those two hard chairs, was difficult to say. I noticed for the first time that there was no clock in that room. Nor was there a calendar on the wall. Even the limited daylight coming through the small recessed window was defeated by the glare of the light-bulb, further isolating the office interior from the world outside. And as long as they offered no excuse or reason for what they failed to do, Tam and Richie would have to remain under Donald's relentless gaze. This was their punishment.

Several minutes seemed to pass before it was over. Eventually

Donald leaned back in his chair and shook his head slowly.

'What are we going to do with you?' he said. They did not even try to answer.

After Tam and Richie had been dismissed, Donald turned to me.

'You'll have to go with them to put Mr McCrindle right. Not a very good start, is it?'

'Not really,' I said. He appeared to be implying that I had played some part in the slackness of Mr McCrindle's fence, a sort of guilt by association, even though I'd only met Tam and Richie about ten minutes earlier.

'While you're there can you also make sure the fence is straight,' Donald added. I had been wondering when he would bring up the question of straightness. Donald was known to have an obsession about it. He could often be seen glancing along a line of posts during the construction process, making sure the alignment was true. Obviously it was better for a fence to be straight, if only for the sake of appearance, but Donald wanted perfection. As Mr McCrindle had demonstrated by his phone call, the main concern of farmers was that their fences should be tight. Without this the restraint of beasts was impossible. We were rushing back to deal with Mr McCrindle's fence because it had gone slack, and for that reason only. I doubt if he had even looked to see if it was straight or not, despite Donald's concern. It most probably was straight, but if for some reason it wasn't, well then what was I supposed to do? Take out all the posts and start again? Donald's pursuit of perfection seemed to be taking things too far. The way he went on anyone would think we were engaged in an exact science. After all, we were only fencing contractors. The process was straightforward.

You put posts in the ground, you stretched wires between them, and then you moved on. That's what we'd done in the last gang I was in. It was repetitive work, but to tell the truth the whole operation was so simple we hadn't even needed a foreman. We just got on with it. And when the fence was finished it was invariably straight, more or less.

Of course, Tam and Richie hadn't helped matters by building a fence that went slack. Apparently they'd been working away at Mr McCrindle's for several days before suddenly returning the previous evening claiming the job was now complete. Donald had estimated the contract would take a week, but they'd come back a day early. The phone call this morning had merely confirmed his belief that they needed closer supervision.

'One more thing,' he added. 'There'll be no need for Richie to drive the truck any more.'

'Why's that then?' I asked.

'It's part of a new policy I've formulated to reduce our insurance costs. Only foremen will drive company vehicles from now on. Richie is banned.'

'Have you told him?'

'Robert has told him,' he replied.

'What about Tam?'

'He's banned by the Constabulary.'

Now that Donald was giving me his full attention, I found myself looking at the top of his desk most of the time, rather than directly at him. He had this way of staring at people for moments on end without blinking, and it was most disconcerting. Even Tam and Richie could be easily reduced under his gaze. When they were out in the fields they looked like wild men, head-bangers with long Viking hair. If it weren't for their rubber wellington boots they'd appear quite menacing. Yet it only took a prolonged stare from Donald to render them meek and mild. During their interrogation about Mr McCrindle's fence they'd both spent most of the time gazing at Donald's typewriter, and now I was doing the same thing. I noticed the sheet of paper in the roller, and upside down I could see three names printed under the heading 'No. 3 Gang'. One of them was mine. As I tried to read the other two names I realized that Donald had stopped talking.

'Banned by the Constabulary?' I repeated.

I thought I caught the first twinkle of a joke coming here, so I grinned and said, 'Oh, yes. Ha.'

Donald just continued gazing at me, so I went outside.

I found Tam and Richie sitting in the truck again, side by side in the double passenger seat, with their arms folded. The pile of equipment didn't look as if it had been touched.

'Right,' I said. 'Do you want to finish sorting this lot out?'

'Not particularly,' Richie replied.

I tried a different approach. 'OK. We'll sort this lot out and then go to Mr McCrindle's.'

'What time are we having our break?' he asked.

'You've just had it,' I replied.

'When?'

'When you had your sandwiches.'

'Oh.'

'Well, can we have a fag first?' said Tam.

'I suppose so,' I said.

'Like one?'

'Oh. Er . . . no thanks. Thanks anyway.'

So we sat in the truck for another few minutes while they smoked two more of Richie's cigarettes.

'Donald got a bit heavy, didn't he?' I remarked after a while.

'Fucking right,' said Richie.

There was a brief silence, then Tam spoke. 'I fucking hate it when he calls us into the office.'

I nodded.

'So what was this Mr McCrindle like then?' I asked.

'He kept sneaking up on us,' replied Tam.

'Did he?'

'Asking questions about the fence all the time. We could never get rid of him.'

'Maybe he found it interesting,' I suggested.

'Huh,' said Tam.

'I thought he was alright,' said Richie. 'He made us a cup of tea one day.'

'Fucking big deal!' snapped Tam. 'He was always interfering. What about when he was watching us behind that tree?'

'Oh,' said Richie. 'I forgot about that.'

'What was that then?' I asked.

'He was spying on us,' said Tam.

'Was he?'

'Then he comes along. "How's it going, boys?"'

'Perhaps he was just trying to be friendly,' I said.

'Too fucking friendly,' said Tam.

They finished smoking.

'So why do you think his fence has gone slack?' I asked.

Tam looked at me. 'What's that supposed to mean?'

'Well,' I said. 'Why do you think it has? I'm just asking, that's all. So we know what tools we'll need.'

'Must be something wrong with the wire,' he said.

'Donald seems to think it's faulty workmanship.'

'He would.'

'But you're saying it isn't.'

'I've just told you it's the wire.'

'So you don't think a post could have come loose then?'

Tam hardened his look. 'Our posts never come loose,' he announced.

'Here's Robert,' said Richie.

Ralph had just appeared from round the corner of the out-buildings, which meant that Robert wasn't far behind. A moment later he came into sight. Without a word from me, Tam and Richie both got out of the truck and disappeared into the store room.

When they were gone Robert came and spoke to me. I noticed he was carrying Richie's Irn-Bru bottle in his hand.

'I had a word with them,' he said.

Yes . . . er . . . thanks,' I replied.

He studied the label on the bottle. 'So they're being alright, are they?'

'Yes, yes,' I said. 'Fine.'

'No problems?'

'No.'

'Are you sure?'

'Certain.'

'Good. We like all our gangs to be balanced.'

He nodded and smiled at Tam and Richie as they emerged again. Then he wandered off, still carrying the empty bottle, followed by Ralph. I watched as they crossed the yard and entered an office adjoining, but separate from, Donald's.

I felt a bit sorry for Robert because he didn't really have enough to do. Ever since Donald had taken over the management of the company, Robert's role had been gradually whittled away. That was why he spent so much time going for walks. These consisted of a vague meander across the fields surrounding the company premises, along a route apparently chosen by Ralph. Afterwards they would come back and Robert would sit in his office again. Nobody was sure what he did in there. He didn't even have a telephone these days. Donald ran the company more or less on his own, setting up contracts, dispatching gangs and so forth. This was done with the utmost efficiency. No more than one gang was allowed 'home' at any one time, to the extent that I'd hardly ever actually set eyes on any other employees. I had no idea where Nos. 1 and 2 gangs were working or when they were expected to return. The company premises, as a result, always seemed quiet. Donald controlled everything and Robert was only kept on hand to perform the occasional duty. His task today, for example, had been to tell Tam and Richie they would shortly be going to England with their new foreman. Whereas Donald chose to impart the news himself that Mr McCrindle's fence had gone slack.

Mr McCrindle had a sloping field. A sloping field! As if a farmer didn't have enough to worry about. It was the curse of his life: always had been. Not only was there a terrible problem with surface water during the winter months, but now all the government drainage grants were beginning to dry up. Worst of all, the bottom part of the field was so steep it was no use to him because his cows wouldn't go down there. And if they did they wouldn't come back!

Mr McCrindle told us all this as we stood at the top of the field wishing he would go away. Tam and Richie had heard it all before, of course, and now they kept slightly aloof, leaving me to deal with him.

'Sounds like you'd be better off with sheep,' I remarked.

Mr McCrindle looked at me. 'Sheep?'

'Yes,' I said. 'With it being sloping, like. They might prefer it.'

'I'm a dairy farmer,' he said. 'What would I want with sheep?'

'Er . . . don't know. Just a suggestion, really.'

The difficulty with talking to Mr McCrindle was that he had very watery eyes which made him look as though he was going to burst into tears at any moment. You felt you had to be very careful what you said to him. I'd only mentioned sheep in a half-hearted attempt to change the subject of conversation. Up until then we'd been talking about Mr McCrindle's new fence, and he'd made it quite clear just how disappointed he was.

'I'm very disappointed, boys,' he kept saying, with a glance at Tam and Richie. 'Very disappointed indeed.'

He'd been onto us ever since the moment we arrived. No sooner had we got out of the truck to survey the situation, than he had come chugging into the field in his van. I would have preferred to have a chance to work out what had gone wrong before he turned up. Maybe have a walk down the fence line to consider our position and prepare ourselves for awkward questions. But, in the event, he was on the scene straight away, so there was nothing I could do.

'It's a very sorry state of affairs,' he said, the tears welling up in his eyes.

Mr McCrindle had every right to be disappointed. He had particularly specified a high-tensile fence, even though it was much more expensive than a conventional one. That was why he had contacted the company in the first place. It specialized in high-tensile fencing and had been a pioneer in developing the technique to its present state. Only best-quality galvanized spring-steel wire and weather-resistant posts were used, every fence being erected by highly experienced personnel. He knew this because it was all outlined in the illustrated company brochure (written by Donald).

Mr McCrindle now surprised me by producing a copy from his inside pocket.

'It says here,' he said, reading aloud. ' "A high-tensile fence should retain its tension for the first five years at least." '

He poked his finger at the line of print. 'See? Five years. Cost me a fortune and it went slack overnight!'

We looked across at the evidence, a line of brand new posts marching off down one side of the field, with all the wires hanging limp.

'No use to man nor beast!' he announced.

Poor Mr McCrindle. I thought he was going to break down in front of me. All he wanted to do was get his cows turned into the field, but he couldn't. Of course he was disappointed! He was a livestock farmer whose new fence had gone slack, and I wanted to put my arm around his shoulder and say, 'There there.'

'Let's see what the problem is then,' I said, striding towards the fence. As I approached I remembered Donald's injunction about checking that it was straight. To do so it was necessary to perform a sort of genuflection at one end of the fence and glance along the line of posts. I was just doing this when I became aware that Mr McCrindle had followed me and was looking puzzled.

'What are you doing?' he asked, as I stood upright again.

'Nothing really,' I replied. 'Just making sure it's straight.'

Behind Mr McCrindle I noticed Tam and Richie exchanging glances.

'What's that got to do with the price of tea in China?' he asked.

'Well . . . I just thought I'd look, that's all.'

'And is it?'

'Take a look for yourself.'

Mr McCrindle stood at the end of the fence and genuflected with a grunt. 'Oh, me bloody back!' He shut one eye, then the other. 'What am I supposed to be lining it up with?'

'Itself.'

I left Mr McCrindle squinting along the line of posts and set off down the fence to see if I could find the fault. Realizing that they were now alone with him, Tam and Richie quickly followed after me.

I inspected every post as I went, to make sure each one was firmly embedded in the ground. They all were. I examined the condition of the wire. It was shining and new, straight from the factory. All the time I was aware of Tam and Richie watching me, watching the tests I carried out on their fence. Eventually we got down to the other end.

'See?' said Tam.

'What?' I said.

'You said a post must be loose.'

'No I didn't. I just wondered why the fence had gone slack, that's all.'

Tam looked at me but said nothing.

'So why has it then?' I asked.

'Mr McCrindle shouldn't have kept interfering.'

'Yeah, alright, but that's no reason . . .'

'Well I don't fucking know!' he snapped. 'I'm not fucking foreman, am I?'

'What difference does that make?' I said, but Tam had already turned and gone stomping off up the field.

I looked at Richie. 'Now what?'

'Tam used to be foreman.'

'When?'

'Until you came along.'

'What, today?'

He nodded.

'I didn't know that,' I said. 'Who was he foreman of?'

'Me.'

'I thought you were both equal.'

'He's been a fencer longer than me . . . or you,' he said.

I sighed. 'It's not my fault. This was Donald's idea.'

'Oh.' Richie was now idly toying with a fence wire.

'By the way,' I said. 'Why do you think it's gone slack?'

'Mr McCrindle kept interfering,' he replied.

Well, maybe, but it looked to me as if the wires simply hadn't been tightened up properly in the first place. The fence bore all the hallmarks of a job that had been rushed in the final stages, and in a way Mr McCrindle probably could be held to blame. Tam had complained earlier about how he was forever sneaking up on them and poking about while they were building the fence. I came to the conclusion that Tam and Richie had simply failed to tighten the wires properly because of their haste to escape the attentions of Mr McCrindle. It was no excuse, but, nevertheless, it was probably the reason.

'Is that what you want me to tell Donald then?' I asked.

'Dunno,' said Richie.

Well I knew, and I could just imagine what Donald would say. After all, the company was hardly going to make a profit on a job that had gone wrong like this. Tam seemed to have conveniently forgotten that it would be me, not him, who would have to report back to Donald. It was me who had to take responsibility for restoring the tension in Mr McCrindle's fence. I could see already that we were going to have to come back again the next day. It had taken so long to get all Tam and Richie's equipment sorted out and straightened up, before driving out to Mr McCrindle's, that the light had already started to fade by the time we got there. At this time of the year the darkness crept up on you so slowly you barely noticed, and it was far too late to start tightening wires now. Which meant we'd have to return tomorrow. All highly inefficient. It wasn't really a job for three men over two days, yet what could I do? I could hardly send Tam and Richie back here unsupervised tomorrow, especially not with Mr McCrindle lurking around. And it seemed unthinkable to split them up and just bring Tam. Or just Richie. As far as I knew that had never been done. Fortunately, Donald seemed to have washed his hands of the Mr McCrindle episode and wanted nothing more to do with it.

As long as I got it sorted out 'before the beginning of next week' he would not intervene. Hopefully, by the time the question of profit and loss came up, Mr McCrindle would be a forgotten name in the accounts.

We found Tam brooding about halfway up the fence. There didn't seem to be any sign of Mr McCrindle anywhere, and we decided he must have cleared off for the time being. So at least we had some respite.

'Got a fag, Rich?' said Tam, as we approached. Richie reached for the lump in his shirt pocket and produced his pack of cigarettes, then fished the lighter out of his jeans. As they lit up I wondered with irritation why he didn't keep them together in the same pocket.

Tam turned to me. 'We'll have to come back tomorrow, will we?'

'Looks like it.'

'That's a cunt, isn't it?'

Yes, I agreed, it was. Dusk was now approaching quickly. I left them smoking and went and stood looking down the steep part of the field into the gloom.

To my dismay I saw Robert coming up the other way. What was he doing there? I turned to warn Tam and Richie, whom I could just see in the fading light. I got their attention, put my finger to my lips, and beckoned them to join me quietly.

'He's come to snoop on us,' murmured Tam.

We could now see that Robert had Ralph with him. It was interesting to watch their progress up the slope. Instead of scrambling alongside the fence, as we had done, Robert was following the 'correct' route for his ascent, taking a very meandering path that gained height gradually in a series of switchbacks. This also suited Ralph, who was getting on in years. However, looking from above, Robert hardly appeared to be getting anywhere at all. First he would move across the slope to the right for several yards, then over to the left, back to the right, and so on. With Ralph plodding behind. It seemed to take for ever. Robert never looked up to see how far he'd got. He just kept his eyes carefully on the ground as he chose his path. It was not until he finally reached the top of the slope that he saw us all standing there watching.

'Good evening,' he said.

I must admit I was impressed by Robert's demeanour. Not only had he just ascended a steep slope without a pause, but he had also come face to face with three people he evidently meant to surprise. Yet Robert greeted us with a casual 'good evening' as though we had been expecting him. A bit of a gent really, although Tam and Richie probably regarded him as 'posh'.

'Everything under control?'

'Yes,' I said. 'We've just got to add the finishing touches tomorrow.'

'Good.'

'Are you going to speak to Mr McCrindle?' I asked.

'No, that's your job,' he replied.

'What about Donald?'

'I'm here on my own account,' he said. 'You need to report direct to him . . . if and when appropriate.'

Then, after a polite nod to Tam and Richie, Robert turned and went back the way he had come, with Ralph trailing after him. Why he'd journeyed all this way to see us remained unclear. If he was merely snooping, as Tam put it, then it was only in a most harmless way because he'd given the fence nothing more than a cursory inspection in passing. He was unfamiliar with the technical side of fencing anyway, and was probably only taking a proprietorial interest in a business he could no longer influence. It was like a powerless head of state paying a visit to foreign subjects about whom he knew little. He stayed a short while just to remind us that he existed, and then he went away again. His role was generally unimportant, and as he disappeared into the gathering dusk I couldn't help feeling sorry for him.

'It's the dog I feel sorry for,' remarked Tam.

When we were convinced Robert had definitely gone the three of us trudged back up the field. We found the truck in the darkness and headed for the gate. On the way out we passed Mr McCrindle's van coming in. He flashed his headlights. I flashed back in a friendly way and we fled.

By the time I'd got home, washed and changed and gone out again, the Leslie Fairbanks evening was in full swing. Leslie Fairbanks had a residency at the Crown Hotel Public Bar. Once a week he performed his musical programme entitled 'Reflections of Elvis' to what seemed to be the entire local population. We lived in a quiet place on the road to Perth, and the Crown Hotel was the only establishment you could get a drink apart from the Co-Op off-licence. It occupied one side of a small square opposite the bank at the top of the main street. Which was, in fact, the only street. I don't think Leslie Fairbanks was his real name: I'd seen him once or twice behind the wheel of a lorry with the words 'L. G. Banks, Road Haulage' stencilled on the side of the cab. Leslie Fairbanks was his chosen stage persona for the nights he appeared with his accordion. Sometimes the show was billed as 'Reflections of Hank' by way of a change, but he always remained Leslie Fairbanks. He generally wore a spangled waistcoat for the occasion. A hundred or so people turned up on such evenings at the Crown Hotel, and they needed to be entertained. Leslie Fairbanks had acquired an amplifier for this purpose, and always spent an hour beforehand setting up his equipment and carrying out a sound check, assisted by a youth in dark glasses. Jock the barman, polishing the surface of his counter, could never for the life of him understand why they had to turn it up so loud. It was more than a man could bear. Jock kept a pair of spectacles on a chain round his neck, and he would frequently peer through them at the tangle of cables running from the low stage to the mixing desk.

'Whatever do they need all those for?' he would ask anyone he thought might listen to him. Nobody did. They came to the Crown to drink, and on the nights Leslie Fairbanks played they just drank more. This was rural Scotland. There was nothing else to do.

The amplified accordion sounded like some endless, mournful dirge as I approached through the drizzle that evening, but the lights of the Crown Hotel were too bright to let that discourage me. Once inside the door a more convivial noise took over, as Leslie Fairbanks's endeavours were augmented by the combined racket of drinks being served, laughter and shouted arguments. The place was packed, bodies pressed against each other in a churning mass of persons bent on enjoying themselves despite the odds. Meanwhile, Jock bawled over the tops of people's heads and kept general order at the bar, assisted when things got especially busy by a girl called Morag Paterson. Sales always increased marginally while Morag was behind the counter, but she was only helping out and most of the time she remained at the other side amongst the customers. Seated on one of the barstools nearby was Mr Finlayson, the greenkeeper at the local golf course. His three sons also drank here. One of them was Tam. He was sitting at a big table with his brother Billy and some of their cohort, so I worked my way across the room. They watched me approach and I saw Billy ask Tam something. Tam nodded, then looked up at me as I joined them.

'Alright to sit here?'

'If you like.'

They made a space for me and I sat down, glancing round. 'No Richie?'

'We're not married, you know,' Tam replied.

'No, I know,' I said. 'I just wondered where he was, that's all.'

Tam looked at me. 'Rich can't come out tonight. He's got to pay the instalment on his guitar.'

'Oh, I didn't know he played the guitar. What sort?'

'You'll have to ask him, won't you?'

'Yeah, 'spose.'

I tried to engage Tam in some conversation about fencing, how many miles he'd done, and where, and so forth, but he didn't seem interested in talking. Judging by the number of empty glasses on the table he'd already had quite a lot to drink before I got there. Also, it wasn't easy competing against the continual din in the background, especially when a loud 'clunk' signalled that a microphone was being plugged into Leslie Fairbanks's amplifier. I shortly became aware of a man's voice, apparently singing. Someone had got hold of a mike from behind the bar, and was standing next to Leslie Fairbanks singing as if his life depended on it. His voice was nasal, to the extent that it sounded as if there was a clothes peg clipped onto his nose. He sang with his eyes shut and his fists clenched, while Leslie Fairbanks followed on the accordion, his head tilted to one side, and a faint smile on his face. He appeared to have no objection at all to being usurped by this floor singer and I began to think it was probably something that happened every week. No one else in the place seemed to take the slightest notice of the new addition on stage. They just carried on drinking and shouting all the louder. This more or less put paid to any further talk, so I entertained myself by lining up empty beer glasses with each other across the table-top, watched with vague interest by Tam. It had been a fairly pleasant evening so far, but things began to change after Morag Paterson came to collect up a trayful of empties. It would probably have been alright if Jock hadn't been too busy to do the job himself. Jock would have parted the crowd roughly and elbowed his way round the tables, grabbing five glasses with each hand and finding something to be grumpy about. Instead it was Morag who appeared, gently leaning over to ask if I'd mind passing the empty glasses. I hardly looked at her, but after she'd gone Tam began to slowly ferment. Several times I caught him staring at me and I had to pretend to be listening intently to Leslie

Fairbanks and his partner, who were now in full flow. Tam had been drinking pints of heavy all night, and as he drained the latest one I thought I heard him say something like 'Well, it's about time ex-foreman Tam Finlayson bought the new English foreman a drink, is it not?'

Whatever his intention had been when he rose to his feet, something must have got to Tam before he got to me, because instead of asking what I would like to drink, he just lunged at me across the table, so that several glasses went over. I leaned back to avoid him and next moment he had reared up and was standing before me yelling 'C'mon, English bastards!' at the top of his voice.

As far as I knew I was the only English person in the place, so I stood up at my side of the table and waited to see what happened. Tam looked like he was about to make another lunge when Billy intervened.

'Tam, no!' he shouted.

'English bastards!' Tam screamed. It was odd the way he kept going on about 'bastards' in the plural. This suggested it was nothing personal.

Then Billy got Tam in a sort of bear-hug and they both toppled sideways onto the floor amongst the seething mass of drinkers. One or two people began jeering playfully.

Leslie Fairbanks, man of the moment, saw what happened but decided to press on during the disturbance, somehow managing to change to a much slower, more soothing tune without anybody noticing. This had the interesting side effect of causing his vocal accomplice to fall temporarily silent. In the resulting calm Tam and his brother resurfaced and were all smiles. Billy said something in Tam's ear and put his arm round his shoulder.

The incident seemed to have been already forgotten by most of the bystanders. Their father, sitting at the bar, had turned round on his stool, vaguely aware of some commotion, but quickly lost interest and began to contemplate his drink again. My glass was amongst those that had been knocked over, and as a result it was now empty. As I forlornly stood it upright on the table, Tam settled down opposite me. Billy sat next to him, a large grin on his face.

'I'm sorry,' said Tam.

'That's OK.'

'No, really. I'm very, very sorry.'

'Yeah, well.'

'C'mere.' Tam reached over the table and clasped my hand. Now he wanted to be my friend, my buddy.

'Like a drink?'

'Go on then.'

As Tam lurched off to the bar Billy said, 'Don't worry about Tam. If he goes like that again just come and get me.'

'Thanks,' I said. 'What am I going to do with him when we get to England?'

Billy just shrugged.

There was a squeal over at the bar. Tam had managed to spill beer across the counter and most of it had gone over Morag Paterson. Despite the squeal she didn't seem particularly upset. In fact, she was laughing. It was my beer, of course, that Tam had spilt, and after a while I realized he wasn't coming back with another one. Eventually I went and bought a drink each for me and Billy. Making sure it was Jock who served me.

Tam was late for work next day, so I sat in the truck with Richie, waiting for him to turn up.

'Go out last night?' I asked.

'Couldn't afford it,' he replied, lighting a cigarette.

'Tam tells me you play the guitar.'

'Well, I'm still learning it really,' he said. 'I've only had it three weeks.'

'What sort is it then?'

'Electric.'

Richie was not being very forthcoming, so I gave up trying to interview him about his hobbies. Instead we sat silently in the cab as it slowly filled with smoke. Eventually Tam arrived, failing to provide any excuse for his lateness, and we set off on what we hoped would be our last trip to Mr McCrindle's. It was imperative we got his fence finished today at all costs, or we'd never hear the last of him.

He was nowhere to be seen when we arrived, which was a good start. He must have been occupied at another part of the farm. While Tam and Richie prepared the wire-tightening equipment I went off to take a measurement of the fence, something we'd forgotten to do the day before. This was simply a matter of running a measuring wheel along the entire length of the fence. A small meter at the side of the device clicked up 513 yards. (Donald had decided not to convert from yards to metres because, as he put it, most farmers were incapable of thinking metrically.) When I got back Tam asked me how long the fence was.

'513 yards,' I told him.

'I'll measure it,' he announced, taking the wheel and setting off down the field. I let him get on with it as there was plenty of time to spare. When he came back the meter read 522. I don't know how he achieved this figure, but I recorded it all the same. Now we could concentrate on getting Mr McCrindle's new fence up to the required level of tension. Tam had elected to do the re-tightening. I didn't protest as it was his fence officially, and he was supposed to be a good judge of torque. I sent Richie down to the bottom of the field to keep an eye on the job from that end, then all I had to do was stand and watch in my capacity as foreman.

The wire-tightening gear consisted of a wire-gripper and a chain winch. Tam began the process by anchoring the winch to the straining post at the start of the fence. This was a substantial piece of timber, dug deep into the ground and supported by a strut at forty-five degrees. He then fixed the gripper to the bottom wire and slowly tightened it by means of a handle which 'walked' link by link along the chain. When he was satisfied with the tension he tied the wire off at the post, and moved up to the next one. As Tam settled into his work the true form of the fence began to appear. The second wire was tightened, then the third, and fourth, each providing a new taut parallel line. It was beginning to look good. At last I could see how perfectly straight the line of posts was, and there was no sign of any weakening of the structure. Tam would pull his handle to the left, re-position his feet and pull to the right, and so on, until, slowly, the correct level of tension was reached. As usual

Tam wore his rubber boots, and he was digging his heels hard into the ground to maintain his balance as he heaved on the handle. At last he came to the top and final wire. This was the most important one, especially in a fence intended to restrain cows, because of their tendency to lean over and eat the grass on the other side. It therefore had to be especially tight. Tam placed the gripper on the wire and carefully cranked the handle one way, then the other. And again one way, then the other. Very slowly now. One way, then the other. He paused.

'That should do it,' I said. The whole fence was humming under the strain.

'I think I'll give it one more,' said Tam. He looked at me for a long moment. 'We don't want it going slack again, do we?'

'Suppose not.'

He planted his feet and began to heave carefully. He really was taking this to the limit this time. It was just as he got the handle about halfway that I noticed Mr McCrindle had joined us. I don't know where he'd come from, but he was now standing directly behind Tam, watching him work. Maybe it was Mr McCrindle's sudden appearance that caused Tam to lose his footing. I'm not really sure, it all happened so quickly. Mr McCrindle said something and Tam seemed to glance sideways. Next thing his balance had gone and he was jerked off his feet. The shock of the change in direction sent the chain snaking upwards for a moment. A moment just long enough for the gripper to release the wire and fly back towards Mr McCrindle. He was still speaking as it hit the side of his head.

It sounded to me like 'Norbert' or maybe 'Noydle'. Whatever he was saying, the words trailed off as Mr McCrindle keeled over. I stepped forward to catch him, and discovered how difficult it can be to hold someone upright when they appear to have stopped trying. So I leant him against the fence.

Mr McCrindle had a very surprised look on his face. His eyes were wide open, but he was, apparently, dead.

3

Tam looked at Mr McCrindle and then turned to me. 'I didn't mean to do that,' he said.

'I know you didn't,' I replied.

'He shouldn't have kept sneaking up on us.'

'Never mind that now.'

Any distant observer of this scene would have probably assumed that the three figures standing by the new fence were in deep conversation about something. In fact, there were only two participants in the conversation.

'What do you think he was saying?'

'Dunno,' said Tam. 'Could've been "Nice work, boys," maybe.'

'Or "Not too tight, Tam",' I suggested. 'I didn't catch the last bit.'

There was a bit of a breeze blowing that day. It rustled a nearby line of trees and caused Mr McCrindle to sway ever so slightly as he stood leaning against the wires.

Tam shivered and zipped up his jerkin.

'Here's Rich,' he said.

We watched as Richie slowly trudged up the field in our direction, glancing every now and then at the fence.

'The top wire's still slack,' he said as he joined us, and then 'Oh, hello, Mr McCrindle.'

When there was no reply he turned and gave me a puzzled frown.

'Tam's just accidentally killed Mr McCrindle,' I explained.

'Oh . . . er . . . oh,' he said, and looked at Mr McCrindle again.

'He must have come to see about getting his cows turned out,' remarked Tam.

We moved Mr McCrindle out of the way and leaned him against the truck so that we could get the fence completed properly. Tam cranked up the top wire and tied it off at the post. I noticed this time he didn't take the tension quite as far as before.

When he'd finished we all stood and regarded the new fence, its wires shimmering in the cold afternoon light.

After a long silence Richie said, 'What are we going to do with Mr McCrindle?'

'Well,' I replied. 'I suppose we'd better bury him.'

This was my first major decision as foreman. Amongst the equipment in the back of the truck was a tool for digging post holes. It was made up of two long-handled spades coupled together to form a pair of tongs. The straining posts which anchored a fence at each end had to be set in deep, narrow holes, and this tool was perfect for the job. If we dug a hole a little deeper and wider than usual, there'd be plenty of room for Mr McCrindle.

'Let Richie dig it,' said Tam. 'He's best.'

With a bashful look of concentration on his face Richie made a cut into the surface, slicing out the turf and placing it to one side. Then he started working into the ground below. Each excavation was the same basic movement. He drove the digger into the bottom of the hole, worked the handles around to get a grip, then closed them together and lifted out the soil, which he deposited on a pile next to him.

I could see that Richie was working much faster than normally would be expected for this sort of task.

'Slow down a bit,' I said. 'You'll wear yourself out.'

He rested for a moment but soon pressed on again. There was no stopping him and he was quickly down into the undersoil. As he delved deeper he had to bend further and further over the hole, until finally he was holding the handles at arm's length and could reach down no more. This was as far as Richie could go, so he stopped and straightened up.

'That's it,' he said.

Tam and I took hold of Mr McCrindle and lowered him into the hole, feet first. We decided to leave his cap on.

Richie had just started shovelling the soil back when Tam made a suggestion.

'Why don't we put a post in as well, to make it look more realistic?'

'We haven't got any spare posts with us,' I said.

'There's one lying in that ditch over there,' he replied.

'What's it doing over there?'

'We had one left over when we built the fence, so we dumped it in that ditch.'

'But you're supposed to take surplus timber away at the end of each job. Donald keeps a record of everything used, you know.'

Tam shrugged.

'Why didn't you take it back?'

'Couldn't be bothered.'

I considered his idea. 'Won't it look a bit funny, a post just standing here on its own?'

'Not really,' he said. 'Somebody might come and hang a gate on it one day.'

'Who?'

'I dunno . . . somebody.'

When I thought about it I agreed he was probably right. There were a lot of posts in the countryside which seemed to be there for no apparent purpose. Some had been waiting many years for a long-forgotten gate to be hung on them. Others started life as the straining posts of fences which, for some reason or other, were never completed. This spare post could join them.

So we fetched it from the ditch where it lay and put it in the hole with Mr McCrindle. Then we back-filled the soil and packed it tight. Tam was very gentle as he replaced the slices of turf and pressed them down with his boot. The finished job looked quite tidy. When we stood back it looked just like an ordinary gatepost. Maybe someone would indeed come along and hang a gate on it one day.

Tam rested his hand on the post. 'Things like this are bound to happen from time to time,' he said.

After that there was nothing left to do, so we put all the gear in the back of the truck and got ready to leave. Already the light was beginning to fade. As dusk approached, the trees stirred and the rising breeze began to sing in the fence wires.

On the way home a thought occurred to me.

'He was dead, wasn't he?'

'I'm sure he was,' said Richie.

'What about his cows?'

'They'll be alright.'

It was time to go to England. No. 3 Gang were being dispatched on Tuesday morning at eight o'clock, and Robert had been given the job of breaking the news officially. I herded Tam and Richie into his office so that he could deliver a short speech.

'Hitherto you've carried out all your work on or near your home ground,' he began. 'This does not mean, however, that any particular precedent is thereby established. Market forces do not recognize feudal boundaries, and if contracts arise further afield then clearly Mohammed must go to the mountain. You also need to bear in mind that building a fence is a combined social and technical exercise . . .'

While Robert went on in this way Tam and Richie stood near the door, looking awkward and nodding each time he paused. I glanced around the room and wondered what he did in here all day long. He had a chair and a desk, but no filing cabinet or telephone, nothing to keep him occupied. In the corner was a low table, under which Ralph lay ignoring the proceedings. Meanwhile, in the adjoining office, a typewriter was being tapped unsteadily. It had always struck me as a bit odd that there was no doorway between Donald and Robert, not even a hatch, so that to communicate with each other they had to go outside into the yard, and back in through the other door.

Presently I noticed that the tapping had stopped. Then I heard quiet footsteps moving behind the partition wall. Evidently Donald was listening in to what was being said. Robert had now turned to the subject of future developments in fencing.

'The high-tension fence is the way forward,' he was saying. 'The prospects of the company depend on it.'

Robert had never really got to grips with the term 'high-tensile', as favoured by Donald, and persisted in quaintly referring to 'high-tension fences'. For this reason he didn't sound very convincing. I suspected that deep down he was a Luddite who secretly preferred old-fashioned conventional fences. Maybe Donald suspected him as well.

As I stood pondering all this I suddenly became aware that Robert had finished his speech and was now sitting behind his desk smiling vaguely.

'Right, thanks for coming in,' he said.

We said it was OK and the three of us trooped outside. As we did so the tapping next door started up again.

The truck was parked across the yard, so we all got in and I reversed it round to the tool shed.

'Got a fag, Rich?' said Tam, and Richie went into the routine with the cigarette pack in his shirt pocket, and the lighter fished out of his jeans. We sat there for a while as they smoked in silence, and then at last Tam spoke.

'What the fuck was Robert talking about?' he said.

Earlier in the day I'd seen Donald separately for my instructions. We were to make preparations for a long journey. It was intended that we should stay away for the entire duration of the contract.

'It's only a few weeks,' he said. 'Then you can come back.'

The company kept a caravan for jobs like this. It was a blue and white model, built to accommodate four persons, and was parked round the back of the timber yard. I asked Tam to go and give the caravan a check while Richie and I sorted out the tools and equipment we'd be needing. Five minutes later Tam came back.

'Right, I've checked it,' he said.

'Oh, good. That was quick.'

'Is that me then?' he asked.

'I suppose so,' I said. 'See you tomorrow. Eight o'clock.'

Sometime after he'd gone I happened to go past the caravan. It was standing in the middle of a huge clump of nettles, and both tyres were flat. I managed to get the door open and have a look inside. It was like a tip. There were cupboards hanging open, mattresses overturned and a bottle of sour milk stood in the sink. This was going to be our home for the next few weeks. I went and found Richie.

'Look at this,' I said. 'I thought Tam said he'd checked it.'

'He probably did.'

It took the two of us more than an hour to get the tyres pumped up and the inside of the caravan fit for habitation. By this time Richie's interest was beginning to flag, so I decided to sort out the rest of the gear myself and let him go home as well. A few minutes after he'd gone Donald came out of the office.

'What time did you tell Tam and Richie tomorrow?'

'Eight o'clock,' I said. 'That's what you told me.'

'Well, there's been a change of plan. I've just had Mr Perkins on the phone and he wants you to be there before dark so he can show you round.'

Mr Perkins was the client in England.

'Can't he show me round next morning? We're bound to arrive after dark, it's miles away.'

'He won't be there,' said Donald. 'He lives somewhere else. You'll just have to leave earlier.'

'How early?'

'I suggest six o'clock.'

'Well, can I use the phone to ring up Tam and Richie?'

'They're not on the telephone.'

'What, neither of them?'

'No.'

'What am I going to do then?'

'You'll just have to go and see them.'

As Donald turned back towards his office I remembered something else I wanted to ask him.

'By the way,' I said. 'Tam seems a bit upset about not being foreman any more. I was wondering if you could make him charge hand, sort of officially?'

'Charge hand?'

'Yes.'

'It's not a grade we recognize.'

'Well couldn't we recognize it just this once?' I tried.

'I'm afraid not,' said Donald, going inside and closing the door behind him.

Richie lived with his parents on a small farm about ten miles away. I had no choice but to get in the truck and drive all the way out there. It was dark by the time I pulled up in the deserted farmyard. A single light shone in the downstairs window. I knocked on the door and after a while Mrs Campbell opened up.

'Oh hello,' I said. 'I've come to tell Richie we've got to go earlier than expected tomorrow morning.'

'I suppose you'd better come in.'

She led me through to the living room where Richie's father was sitting in front of a stick fire.

'Richard's got to go off early tomorrow,' said Mrs Campbell.

'I see,' replied her husband, looking at me. 'I'll just have to do the cows myself.'

Richie's mother disappeared into the depths of the house. Mr Campbell continued looking at me for some time.

'So you're the new foreman?' he said.

'Yes, that's right.'

'I see,' he said, and turned back towards the fire. He was seated in a deep armchair with flat, square sides. Beside it was another armchair, identical and at present empty. I assumed this was Mrs Campbell's. Between them was a small three-legged table. There were some lumps of coal waiting in a bucket next to the fireplace, but at the moment Richie's father was burning sticks. On the shelf above the hearth a clock ticked slowly. The crackle of the flames and the ticking were the only sounds to be heard. I tried without success to imagine an electric guitar being learnt in this house.

After a while Mrs Campbell came back in. 'Richard's just getting ready to go out,' she said. 'Will you have a cup of tea while you wait?'

'Er, no. Thanks anyway,' I replied. 'I just wanted to tell him about leaving early, that's all. I'll have to go soon.'

Mr Campbell looked up at me over the rim of his glasses. 'You'll have a cup of tea.'

I agreed that I would have a cup of tea, and Mrs Campbell withdrew to the kitchen. Behind the two armchairs was a tall oak dresser, and on one of the shelves I noticed a framed picture of a small boy adrift in a rowing boat. The black and white photograph had been taken years before, but the small boy was undoubtedly Richie. There was also a photo of someone I took to be Mr Campbell in his younger days. I glanced at the older version sitting in the armchair. For some reason Richie's father reminded me of Mr McCrindle.

After a few minutes Mrs Campbell returned with the tea, and a tiny cake. I was on my second cup when Richie at last emerged from the back of the house. His mother had said he was getting ready to go out, but I could see no difference in his appearance except that his hair was now washed and shiny, and his wellingtons had been replaced by cowboy boots. I told him the news. He sat down in a hard chair on the opposite side of the fireplace to the bucket of coal.

'Have you told Tam?' he asked.

'I'll tell him in the pub later,' I said.

'What time?'

'Six.'

He looked glum. 'I was going out tonight.'

'And me,' I said. 'This was Donald's idea.'

'I'll have to do the cows myself,' said Mr Campbell again.

After a few more ticks of the clock I showed myself out, leaving Richie and his parents sitting in silence before their stick fire. When I got outside the door I stopped for a moment and listened. Nothing. Somewhere in a nearby field a cow lowed, but there was no other sound. In total darkness I found the truck and drove off.

So this was the life of a foreman. I seemed to be spending most of my time ferrying pieces of information around, in the dark, on behalf of Donald. Tomorrow I had to lead Tam and Richie into exile in England. Tonight, though, the lights of the Crown Hotel offered some consolation.

Word had apparently got round that Tam was going to England. Several people had turned up especially.

'You'll be back by Christmas, I hope?' said Jock.

'Better be,' replied Tam, glancing in my direction.

I shook my head. 'Don't look at me.'

'Send us a postcard, won't you?' said Morag Paterson.

This seemed unlikely to me, but Tam said something polite, and she smiled.

He indicated my glass. 'Pint of heavy?'

'Thanks.'

Sitting further along the bar was Tam's father. He spent a lot of time in the Crown Hotel at this time of year since there was little to do at the golf course after dark. I'd hardly noticed him during the evening, sitting there alone. He seemed to be in a world of his own, seriously involved with his beer glass and nothing else. Now, though, he began to take an interest in the conversation going on nearby. He sat up straight and stared along the counter.

'Who's going to England?'

'Oh for fuck sake,' said Tam.

'Who's going to England?' repeated Mr Finlayson, raising his voice.

'Me.'

'When?'

'Tomorrow.'

His father started up sharply. 'Well you might have told me!'

Tam began to ignore him, gathering up a clutch of pints.

'I said you might have told me!' The words were now loud and angry. Morag Paterson turned away and talked to a friend, while Jock busied himself washing glasses at the other end of the bar.

'C'mon,' Tam murmured to me, and we made our way over to a table where Billy was waiting. There were now a few heads turned. I expected Mr Finlayson to pursue us across the room, but instead the shouting quickly subsided as we joined Billy and sat down.

'What was Dad on about?' asked Billy.

'Nothing,' said Tam. 'Pay no attention to him.'

They seemed to quickly forget the incident. This was evidently

supposed to be a sort of send-off for Tam and they had some
important drinking to do. I hadn't yet got round to telling him
we were going off at six the next day: I didn't want to spoil his
evening. I chose my moment when I was helping him to collect
some drinks from the bar, three or four pints later. He swayed
a little.

'That's alright,' he said. 'No problem.'

'Oh . . . er . . . right,' I said. 'Good. I'll pick you up in the
morning then.'

Tam was smiling now. 'Can you give us a sub until we get
paid?'

'Ant got any money,' I replied.

'Donald gave you a sub,' he said. 'Hundred pounds.'

'That was a float, not a sub,' I explained. 'To cover out-of-
pocket expenses.'

Donald had made a big thing that morning about the difference between a float and a sub. The hundred pounds float
he'd given me was meant to cover the cost of fuel and sundry
necessities, as opposed to a sub, which was actually the same
as a loan. Loans were against company policy and therefore
had to be refused. It seemed that Donald had successfully indoc-
trinated me. I explained my position through the haze that
swam between Tam and me.

'Go on,' he said. 'Give us a sub.'

'Can't.'

He changed tack. 'Go on . . . as a friend.'

This was all Mr Perkins's fault. If he hadn't insisted we got
to his place before nightfall tomorrow then I wouldn't be having
to bribe Tam to get up early in the morning. Yes, bribe! There
was no other word for it. Tam knew it was an unreasonable

demand, especially on his last night at home. He was trying a
bit of moral blackmail. Yes, he would get up early, but only if
I lent him some money.

'I thought Rich lent you some money yesterday,' I tried.

'Spent it,' he said.

It occurred to me that while we were away Donald would
be sending our wages in cash every week. They'd be addressed
to me, which meant I could simply deduct what Tam owed me
before I handed them over. So I decided it would be safe to
lend him a tenner. He spent most of it that night. Last thing I
saw of him he was promising, SWEARING!, to be ready at six
next morning.

'I'll be there. You can count on me,' he said, reeling off
towards Morag Paterson.

Next day I hauled myself out of bed, took breakfast and got
into the truck about a quarter to six. I was not confident. I'd
told Richie six o'clock, but I got to his place a little later to give
him more time. To my surprise he was waiting at the gate with
his bag.

'I've been here twenty minutes,' he complained.

It was still dark when we arrived at the entrance to the golf
course and turned up a gravel track. The course itself was set
back from the road behind a grove of larch trees. Where the
trees ended we came to a wooden two-storey house with a low
white paling. A sign on the gate said GREENKEEPER. This was

where Tam lived, but there were no lights on. I turned off the engine and groaned.

'I knew he wouldn't be ready.'

'Give him a chance,' said Richie.

I bibbed the horn. We waited. Suddenly a hand came in through the window on Richie's side and seized him by the throat.

4

Another hand followed, grabbing his hair. I wound my window shut.

'One false move and I'll pull your fucking head off,' said a voice in the darkness.

Richie stayed quite still. The two hands slowly twisted his head sideways towards the window, forcing him to look outside. 'Oh hello, Mr Finlayson,' he said. 'Is Tam up yet?'

'Who wants him?' said the voice.

'It's me. Rich.'

The hands let go of Richie, and next moment Mr Finlayson thrust his head in through the window.

'How are you?' he said.

'Fine,' I murmured.

'Glad to hear it,' he replied.

'Nice golf course you've got here,' I added.

'How do you know that?' he asked.

'Sorry?'

'What are you sorry about?'

'Er . . . nothing,' I said.

'Is Tam up yet?' repeated Richie.

'I'll see. Wait here.' Mr Finlayson stalked off into the night.

'What did he mean?' I asked.

'It's still dark,' said Richie.

We watched the outline of the house. Any moment a light would appear in one of the windows. Then Tam would come out and we could get going. So I thought anyway. Instead, nothing happened. There was no sign of any movement, and now Tam's father had disappeared as well. I wondered what he was doing wandering around at this time of the morning, in the dark.

'C'mon, Tam,' I muttered. The house remained silent. I was beginning to get fed up with this, and bibbed the horn again. As the sound faded away my door suddenly flew open and a face came in roaring 'RAAAAAAAAH!!'

Out of the corner of my eye I saw Richie jump in his seat.

'Got you!' shouted Tam. 'Got you both! RAAAAH!!'

'Fuck sake,' said Richie. He moved over to let Tam in next to him.

'Sorry I'm late,' said Tam. 'I've been shagging Morag Paterson all night.'

Richie looked impressed. 'Have you?'

Tam grinned at him. 'Fucking right I have.'

'So she's still inside the house is she?' I asked.

'What? . . . oh, er, no . . .' said Tam. 'Not really, no.'

After all this running round picking up Tam and Richie, we now had to go back to the company yard and collect the caravan.

'Have you got food and stuff?' I asked them, as we set off back down the golf course track.

'No,' they both replied.

'Well, have you had breakfast?'

'I had a cup of tea,' said Richie.

It was still dark when we got back to the yard, and the whole place was silent. It seemed important to get away as quickly as possible. Donald lived on the premises and occupied the house at the end of the yard. Although there were no lights on, there was no doubt that he was awake, listening to our movements. If we took too long with our preparations there was a chance he would come out to ask what was causing the delay. It was only the thought of Donald making a sudden appearance that made Tam and Richie move with any sense of haste at all. As it was, the caravan proved particularly difficult to hook onto the tow bar. The ball-hitch mechanism seemed to have gone rusty and jammed up since it was last used. Only after a prolonged struggle in the darkness, each of us giving urgent whispered orders to the others, did we finally get it engaged.

'By the way,' I said quietly to Tam. 'I thought you told me you checked the caravan yesterday?'

'I did,' he replied.

'Well, how come both tyres were flat?'

He walked round and pressed his boot against the tyres. 'They look alright to me,' he announced.

After what seemed ages we finally got going. I calculated that we had about ten hours to get to our destination before nightfall, as requested by Mr Perkins. It sounded like quite a long time, but we had several hundred miles to go and were starting off on back roads, towing a caravan. We needed to average forty miles per hour all the way. It hardly sounded anything at all, but I slowly came to realize that it was an almost impossible target. Daylight had come long before I would admit it and turn the headlights off. Our so-called early start had ticked away, and that old wreck of a caravan we were towing wasn't going to help us make up time. Still, we settled into the journey well enough. I knew it wouldn't be long before one of them would remember he hadn't had any breakfast, and they'd start going on about stopping somewhere to eat. For the time being, however, they seemed content to smoke Richie's cigarettes. Which is how we came to have a discussion about litter. Tam said, 'Got a fag, Rich?' and Richie went through the ritual with the cigarette pack in his shirt pocket and the lighter in his jeans. He had particular trouble getting at the lighter as he sat squashed between me and Tam, and squirmed all over the place as he tried to fish it out, knocking my elbow several times. They were the last two cigarettes in the pack, so afterwards Tam chucked it out of the window.

I said, 'You shouldn't drop litter, you know.'

'Why not?' said Tam.

'Well,' I replied. 'You know. It looks bad, doesn't it? Spoils the countryside and everything.'

'That's a load of shite and you know it,' he said.

'No it isn't,' I said. 'You can't just go chucking rubbish all over the place.'

'You can if you want,' said Tam. 'All this stuff about litter is just English pathetic . . .' He trailed off, and then started again. 'This is Scotland. You're in Scotland and these mountains have been here millions of years. It doesn't make any difference, a few fag packets for fuck sake. That's just English fucking pathetic shite.'

'He's right,' said Richie.

'Yeah . . . I suppose so,' I said.

I couldn't see any mountains.

Sometime later we passed the sign welcoming you to Scotland if you were coming the other way.

'Where are we going?' said Tam.

'Take a look in the folder,' I replied.

Donald always gave us a folder to take on each job, and the previous day he had prepared one containing Mr Perkins's details. It lay on the metal shelf below the dashboard. In it were an address, a road map, an inventory (what we needed to build Mr Perkins's fence), and a field plan (where we would build it). Also a projected completion date. Tam reached for the folder and pulled out a handful of papers, which he studied for a few moments.

'Fuck,' he muttered, and thrust them back inside. Thus, in one movement, Tam transformed Donald's neat file into a crumpled wedge. Richie now took the papers and leafed through them.

'Upper Bowland,' he said at length.

'Upper Bowland?' said Tam. 'Is that the name of the place?'

'Yep,' said Richie, putting the folder back on the shelf. And with that their curiosity subsided. Tam and Richie sat quietly side by side in the double passenger seat, watching the road ahead as we drove into England.

I was breaking the legal speed limit for towing a caravan, and the light was beginning to fade, as we entered the county of Hereford and Worcester. If we had had more time we could have stopped briefly in one of the many towns we'd passed and stocked up on food at a reasonable price in a supermarket, and even checked out promising pubs for future visits. Instead, we had to press on. We'd been pressing on all day. I'd flogged that truck along all sorts of motorways and 'A' roads in my effort to get to Upper Bowland on time. We'd stopped only once, and that was for breakfast hours ago. It had emerged then that Tam had come away without any money at all. In fact, he had very little of anything. The remains of his personal set of fencing tools were somewhere in the back of the vehicle. With him that morning he appeared to have brought just the clothes he worked in, plus a spare pair of jeans and his cowboy boots, all jammed into a small haversack. Richie seemed to be slightly better kitted out, but neither of them had organized any food for while we were away, and now Tam had revealed he had no money either. Richie said he would pay for Tam's breakfast, and seemed to have no objection to subsidizing him for the time being. Which suited me. I looked at the amount of egg, bacon, sausage, tomato, beans, fried slice and mushrooms Tam consumed, and wondered how long Richie would put up with the arrangement.

As I said, that was hours ago. Now we were working our

way along a quiet 'B' road, and it was getting late. I pulled over and checked Donald's map.

'According to this we're looking for a turn-off on the right,' I said.

Not that I expected to get much show of interest from Tam and Richie. They had spent the entire journey gazing silently through the windscreen, smoking from time to time, and taking turns to nod off next to me. I don't think they had any idea what part of England we were in, nor did they care. It was all the same to them. Now that the end of the journey seemed to be getting nearer, however, they began to pay attention again.

I switched on the headlights, which meant, of course, that we hadn't made the deadline. As we drove on we started talking about Mr Perkins. We decided that he was probably waiting at his gate at this very moment, and when we got there he would accuse us of being late, and not making any effort to arrive earlier.

'I expect he's already been on the phone to Donald,' said Tam.

Yes, we all agreed, he probably had.

'Cunt,' said Richie.

Just then we passed a sign on our left which said 'Lower Bowland 3 miles'. I ignored the turn-off and carried on.

'BOWLAND!' shouted Tam. 'That was it back there. You missed the turning!'

'That was Lower Bowland,' I replied. 'We want Upper Bowland.'

'Upper Bowland will be above Lower Bowland, won't it?' he said.

Now Richie joined in. 'Upper Bowland is back there. We've just passed the sign.'

'Upper Bowland is on the right,' I insisted, pressing on and speeding up. No right turning appeared, not for miles. But we kept passing turn-offs for Lower Bowland on the left, and each time Tam and Richie would point out how many miles it was. Lower Bowland was starting to get further away, and there was still no sign of a right turn. I was beginning to lose confidence when suddenly I saw a small lane on the right. There was no signpost but I turned off anyway, and heard Tam murmur something to Richie. This lane seemed to go on and on for ever, but finally, to my relief, the headlights lit up a roadsign: UPPER BOWLAND.

'There you are,' I said. 'You should have had more trust in me.'

'Luck,' said Tam. 'You were lost.'

I pulled up just beyond the roadsign. There was nothing here. No shop, no pub, no houses. Only a farm entrance.

'Hello there,' said a voice in the gloom.

'Mr Perkins?' I said.

'Yes. You found us alright then?'

'Er . . . yes,' I replied.

'Right, well I'd better show you round before it gets any darker. Follow me.'

A figure moved ahead of the truck and began walking up the farm track, and we followed, just keeping him in the beam of the headlights. When we got into the farmyard he showed us where we could park the caravan, and also where the outside tap was. There was a single light on in the kitchen of the farm-house, but it was difficult to see anything clearly, and I never got a proper look at Mr Perkins. He seemed alright though, and hadn't complained about anything so far.

'You're not Scottish?' he said.

'No,' I replied. ' 'Fraid not.'

'But it is a Scottish firm, isn't it? I used them because they said they specialized in high-tension fencing.'

'High-tensile,' I corrected. 'Yes, that's right, we do.'

'But you're not Scottish?'

'No. Sorry. Those two are. I'm not.'

'I see,' he said.

Tam and Richie were somewhere nearby in the shadows. I noticed they hadn't spoken since we arrived, and after un-hitching the caravan were just standing around doing nothing. They needed some instructions, so I gave them some.

'Can you jack up the caravan and connect the gas while I go with Mr Perkins?'

I got into the truck for a moment to get Donald's file. This only took a few seconds, but when I got out again Mr Perkins was standing in the doorway of the caravan talking to Tam and Richie. Then he stepped out and joined me.

'Is there something particular you want to show me?' I asked.

'Yes, along here,' he said, leading me out of the yard and further up the farm track. It was now total darkness. The moon, however, was out.

When we had gone some distance Mr Perkins said, 'I asked your friends if they'd like a cup of tea, but I think there was a bit of a misunderstanding.'

'What did they say then?' I asked.

'They didn't really say anything,' he replied.

We walked for a few more minutes, and then stopped at the top of the track.

'Now this is our hill,' said Mr Perkins.

I was aware of something looming nearby, but could see nothing.

'We want you to divide it into four quarters with your fences. For lambing, you see. We've gone into sheep.'

All this I knew already. I'd read the details yesterday in Donald's file.

'Is there anything else?' I asked.

'No, that's it,' said Mr Perkins. 'I just wanted to show you where the hill was.'

This was what I'd done ten hours' hard driving for. To be shown a hill. I'd seen from the map that this was the only hill of any size for miles around. It was one of those hills that you get here and there in the countryside, thrust up by some geological accident millions of years ago and responsible for the term 'rolling landscape'. But Mr Perkins obviously didn't think I'd be able to find it on my own.

'Right. That's fine. Thanks very much,' I said, and for a few moments I stood with this stranger I could hardly see, looking into the blackness.

'Well, I'd better be off now,' he said at last, and we walked back down to the farmyard. As we passed the caravan I could see two red glow-worms moving silently inside where Tam and Richie sat smoking in the dark. I said goodbye to Mr Perkins and he locked up the farmhouse before going off in his car. Then, with a sinking feeling, I went to the caravan. We must have forgotten to bring the gas bottle. That was why they were sitting in the dark.

'Go on then,' I said. 'Tell me the bad news.'

'What?' said Tam.

'We've forgotten the gas bottle.'

'What are you talking about? We've just connected it.'

'Well, don't you want the lights on?' I asked.

'We're going out, aren't we?'

'Where?'

'The pub.'

'But it's only quarter past five,' I said.

'Oh . . . is it?'

Yes, it was only a quarter past five, and I wondered for the first time what we were going to do at night now that it was beginning to get dark so early. I also realized that, for tonight at least, I was going to have to share some of my food with Tam and Richie. Tomorrow we would have to go and get them stocked up properly. In the meantime we lit the lamps of the caravan. There was an electric striplight at one side, which was supposed to be powered by a cable led out through the window. However, this striplight made such a loud buzzing noise when it was turned on that we hadn't even bothered to bring the cable with us, and were relying on gas lamps only. They were barely adequate, but to tell the truth there was not much worth lighting up. This caravan had been used as a home for itinerant fencers for years, and was, more or less, a wreck. There was a bunk bed in the corner which Richie had claimed. He was already lying in the top half still wearing his wellingtons, and his bag lay on the bit underneath. I seemed to have been given the bed opposite Richie, while Tam was on the one opposite the sink. Next to the sink was a gas cooker, which we lit to make a pot of tea (though we had no milk).

While the kettle boiled I said, 'What did Mr Perkins come and say to you then?'

'He asked if we wanted some tea,' replied Tam.

'Well, why didn't you say yes?' I said. 'That would have been nice. I could have done with a cup of tea when we got here. And I bet he had some milk.'

'Expect he did.'

'Why didn't you say yes then?'

'Because we're not tinkers,' said Tam, giving me a look.

After I'd fed them some canned beans, we arranged ourselves in our three corners with little left to do. Richie had brought his cassette player with him, which he attempted to play powered by batteries only. The batteries were not new, and started to struggle halfway through the Black Sabbath tape Richie had chosen. The sound of Richie's tapes slowly being stretched in an under-powered cassette player was to become a familiar background noise over the coming weeks.

'What else have you got, apart from Black Sabbath?' I asked, after a while.

Richie shuffled his small stack of cassettes. 'Maiden, Motörhead, Saxon.'

I soon came to the conclusion that Tam was right. We would have to go out. I had another look at Donald's road map. This was actually a photocopied page from an atlas. Donald had marked out our route with a green felt-tip pen. At the end of the green line was Upper Bowland, which had turned out to be nothing more than a signpost. A few miles further along the main road, however, the map indicated some kind of settlement. Also the letters PH, for public house. Well, that was hopeful anyway. By this time it had ticked round to seven o'clock and I knew Tam would soon start up again about going to the pub. Richie was lying on his bunk reading a paperback book he had found in one of the cupboards, *An Early Bath for Thompson* by A. D. Young.

'When are we going out?' said Tam.

'There's a pub about five miles from here,' I replied.

Richie instantly put his book away and swung down from his bunk. He took off his wellingtons and put on his cowboy boots. Meanwhile, at the other end of the caravan, Tam was doing the same thing. A moment later they were both standing by the door looking at me.

'You're ready then, are you?' I said.

As I heaved myself off my bed and put the map away Tam said, 'Can I have a sub until we get paid?'

'I lent you some last night,' I said. 'You haven't forgotten, have you?'

'No, no,' he replied. 'But I need some for tonight.'

'And for buying food tomorrow,' I added.

'That as well,' he said.

So I lent him some more money, we went out, and Tam and Richie spent their first evening in an English pub. The Queen's Head, it was called. I don't know quite what they expected, but I knew exactly what it would be like. It came as no surprise to me that there were only about six people inside, and that they all looked towards the door as we entered, me first, then Tam, then Richie.

'Good evening!' boomed the landlord from behind the bar. 'Three pints, is it?'

'Er . . . alright,' replied Tam.

Richie and I went and sat down at a table in the corner,

leaving Tam to pay for the drinks. Then I thought of something and went back to the counter.

'Can we have straight glasses, please?' I said. Tam glanced at me.

'Don't you want tankards?' said the landlord, booming again.

As I suspected, he had already started pouring the beer into dimpled tankards with handles.

'No thanks,' I said.

'Most people want tankards,' he announced.

'Straight glasses if you've got them, please.'

'Right you are,' he said, transferring the beer into proper straight glasses. I went and sat down. A few moments later Tam came over with the beers.

'Tankards,' he said, grinning. The landlord didn't seem to hear him.

'Where is everybody?' said Richie.

'Too early,' I explained. 'There might be a few more in about ten o'clock.'

'What time does it shut, then?'

'Eleven.'

'What?!'

'You're lucky. They used to shut at half ten.'

'For fuck sake,' said Tam.

So there we sat, at a table in the corner, while the locals played darts and no doubt wondered who we were.

In the morning I looked out of the caravan window and saw our future piled up on the other side of the farmyard.

'Look at that lot,' I said.

Tam and Richie, half-awake, leaned on their elbows and peered round the shabby curtains. The materials for the fence had been delivered by lorry a few days prior to our arrival, and all the posts and rolls of wire were there in a huge untidy stack.

'Fuck sake,' said Tam. 'We're going to be here for ever.'

It looked as if the lorry driver had just reversed into the yard and tipped the whole lot out. There were straining posts, pointed posts and struts all mixed up with each other. It was odd that Mr Perkins had not said anything. Maybe he thought it was common practice just to dump all the stuff like this. Donald would have been most dismayed if he had seen it. Not his way of doing things at all.

We sat on our respective beds drinking tea (no milk), and considered starting work.

I decided that Tam and I would sort out all the gear while we sent Richie off to buy their food supply. It was clear that I would have to ignore unilaterally Donald's driving ban on Richie if we were going to get anything done at all.

I suppose it must have been about half past eight when Richie drove off. He and Tam had put together a basic shopping list, and I'd also mentioned we would need milk. So all he had to do was find a shop, buy the groceries, and come back.

By ten o'clock Tam and I had made deep inroads into the pile and it was beginning to look a bit more orderly and Donald-like. We stopped for a cup of tea. With a bit of luck Richie would turn up any minute with some milk to put in it. He didn't. We started work again, and I realized that we were now continually listening for the sound of the truck approaching in the distance. Tam, meanwhile, kept walking to the gateway and looking down the track towards the main road.

'Where do you think Rich is?' he kept saying.

I could see it was beginning to affect his work. He was supposed to be throwing posts down from the pile for me to catch, but his aim was starting to go astray. I had made the cardinal error of separating Tam and Richie. It was only for a short while, but I could see Tam wouldn't be able to function normally until Richie got back. Besides, we needed the truck to shift the materials up to the foot of the hill. This sorting out in the farmyard was really only meant to be a 'starter' job to get us in the swing of things, two hours' work at the outside. If Richie didn't come back soon the day would be lost. We had got to the point of meaninglessly checking off Donald's inventory when he finally returned.

'That took a long time,' I said, as he got out of the truck.

'I know,' he replied. 'I couldn't find a shop.'

'Wasn't there one near that pub?'

'I went the other way.'

The sinking feeling was beginning to return.

'But there weren't any shops the other way,' I said. 'That's the way we came yesterday.'

'I know,' he said. 'I've been miles.'

'So what did you do in the end?'

'Came back.'

There was a pause. 'What . . . you haven't got anything?'

'No.'

There was little more to say on the subject, so we loaded up the truck with posts and wire, and went up to the hill. It was a bare, treeless place, covered with a layer of turf and populated by sheep, which roamed around, grazing here and there. Mr Perkins wanted us to divide it into four quarters, so the final appearance would resemble a hot cross bun. Therefore the first thing we had to do was halve it. Donald had been down to survey the job in advance, and he'd put marker pegs in the ground where the fences were to start and finish.

This first fence would run right over the top of the hill, and needed a straining post at either end. I gave Tam and Richie the task of doing one each. Then I took the shopping list and went to get their supplies for them. As expected, I found a general store about a hundred and fifty yards from the Queen's Head. The whole trip took thirty-five minutes, which should have given Tam and Richie enough time to put their posts in the ground.

I parked at the bottom of the hill and walked round to Tam's end. There was a half-dug hole but no Tam. I carried on round to Richie's end. The two of them were standing by Richie's post, which was complete, having a smoke.

'Just getting a fag off Rich,' said Tam as I approached.

At that moment it struck me we were probably going to be at Upper Bowland a bit longer than Donald had predicted.

All fences had to be straight. This was our mission. Donald had drawn them as straight lines on his plan: therefore, they also had to be straight in real life. Even fences that went right over the top of a hill. Once the first two straining posts were ready, the next job was to stretch a wire between them. This would give us a straight line to work from. We wanted to bisect the hill perfectly, so I asked Tam to go and stand at the top and act as a sighting point. Then Richie loaded a coil of wire onto an unwinder, and began towing out the first strand. This unwinder resembled a small windmill. It turned slowly as Richie made his way up the hill, dragging the wire behind him, and I stood by watching for possible snags. Which required great patience. Each coil contained a quarter of a mile of wire, and I didn't expect him to move particularly quickly. I was quite content to clock his progress as the coil steadily unwound. As he approached Tam at the summit I could tell he was flagging. The unwinder had been turning at a slower and slower rate, and when he got to Tam it stopped altogether.

I waited.

They were discussing something. I wondered what they were talking about, my two colleagues at the other end of the wire. Plotting my overthrow? Probably not. More likely 'Got a fag, Rich?'

Another moment and the unwinder began to move again as Richie continued across the top of the hill and disappeared from my view. Steadily it turned, gradually gaining speed when he started his descent and gravity took over. Soon it was spinning like a whirligig, which meant Richie had taken off at a run down the other side of the hill and was relying on the wire's drag to hold him back and stop him breaking his neck. Suddenly the coil ran out and I watched the tail end go snaking up the hill. The unwinder spun silently to a halt. I assumed Richie had arrived safely at the bottom. Then I loaded another coil onto the unwinder and set off towing the new wire behind me. I found the end of Richie's wire halfway up the hill and tied mine to it with a special fencer's knot. Now we had a continual length of wire running right over the summit of the hill. As soon as it was secure at Richie's end I could pull it tight and we would have our straight line. I glanced up at Tam. Could he see Richie from where he was standing? Probably not. He'd have to walk across the top of the hill to have a look, but this didn't seem to have occurred to him. He was just gazing into space. I shouted to get his attention, but my voice didn't carry far enough. This problem of communication along the fence was nothing new. Donald had considered supplying gangs with walkie-talkies to help make the process more efficient, but then decided that they were 'open to abuse' and abandoned the idea. I lost count of the times I had been at one end of a fence trying to pass instructions to the person at the other. Having a hill between me and Richie made the matter worse.

I suppose it was my fault really. I should have set up some sort of pre-arranged signal before he went off.

I wondered what Tam was staring at. Maybe nothing. Maybe he had been standing there so long his mind had just gone off the job. Meanwhile, I had no idea at all whether Richie had fixed the wire at the other end.

'TAM!' I shouted at the top of my voice.

No response.

Again 'TAM!! You deaf fucker!'

This time he turned towards me. I shrugged at him, meaning 'What's happening?'

He shrugged back. Now what was that supposed to mean? All I wanted him to do was go and have a look down at Richie, come back and give me a signal. But he just stayed where he was. I made a pointing gesture. Still he did not move, apart from shrugging again. I was very reluctant to go up the hill myself, him being already up there. It was such a waste of energy. We were all going to have to go up and down that hill a good many times before this job was finished. All the pointed posts that formed the main body of the fence were going to have to be lugged up there by hand because it was too steep for the truck. Then there would be the rest of the wires to tow out and fix. All in all a lot of to-ing and fro-ing, and I could see no point in me going right up the hill just to ask Tam what Richie was doing. I didn't want to call Tam down yet either: he had to keep an eye on the wire when it was pulled tight to make sure it didn't get caught anywhere and go out of line.

I waved my arm again. Aha! Something had got through to Tam at last, and he set off walking away from me over the top of the hill. I waited a few minutes while he was out of sight. Soon, I thought, he would come back and give me a signal that everything was OK. I continued waiting. He didn't come back.

Eventually, I decided to walk round the bottom of the hill to see if Richie's end was ready. When I got there it came as no real surprise to find he had gone.

My fault again. I was foreman, so I should have organized it better. I looked up the slope but could see no sign of Tam either.

It seemed like a good time to call it a day. The light was failing anyway. By the time I got back to the caravan it was dark. Again they were sitting inside, unseen apart from the glow of their cigarettes.

'Now what?' I said.

'What?' said Richie.

'You haven't lit the lamps.'

'Oh,' he replied. 'No. Couldn't be bothered.'

We talked of going to the Queen's Head again that night. The previous evening, as I foretold, the pub hadn't started to fill up until half past ten. The customers had been mainly blokes, but just before last orders two young women had turned up. They were obviously local girls, you could tell by the way they were greeted when they came in. They took no notice of us three whatsoever. Nevertheless, Tam and Richie decided that 'we' had a 'chance', so for the time being the Queen's Head would remain our drinking base.

'Shame the beer's so weak,' said Richie.

'Weak,' repeated Tam, looking at me. 'Made by weaklings.'

Before we went out for the evening I wanted to have a shave. I filled a kettle with water from the outside tap and put it on to boil. Shaving was part of the downside of being an itinerant fencer. It wasn't too bad if we were at a farm where they kept cows. There was always lots of hot water available in the dairy: something to do with hygiene. Sheep, however, were different. The animals were left to their own devices for much of the time, and absentee farmers like Mr Perkins didn't even live at the place. The only thing on tap was cold water, and if someone wanted to wash and shave they had to boil it themselves. Tam and Richie didn't seem very interested in washing, not on week-days anyway. And they soon got fed up waiting while I had a shave, because the delay meant they couldn't go out yet.

'How long are you going to be?' said Richie, as I poured the boiling water into a bucket.

'Ten or fifteen minutes,' I replied. He grunted and reached for his copy of *An Early Bath for Thompson* for a brief read.

Meanwhile, Tam had nothing to do.

'Why don't you clear that up?' I suggested, nodding towards some baked beans that had been on the floor since last night. They were there because the can opener that came with the caravan was worn out. Richie had attempted to open some beans and the opener got stuck halfway round the lid and refused to go any further. At this point Tam took over the operation, and removed the contents with his wood chisel. Some, however, had gone on the floor. When I went to the general store I asked Tam and Richie if they wanted to go thirds each on a new can opener. They both said no, so I bought myself one and put it in my cupboard. Also in my cupboard were one plate, one cup and a knife and fork, which I washed separately and put away. We were now on our second day in the caravan and Tam and Richie obviously weren't going to do any washing up. All the other plates, pans and cutlery had already been used, and were now stacked in the sink, which, by the way, had no plug. Tam said it was 'pathetic' when I did my own washing up and not theirs. Earlier this evening he asked to borrow my new can opener. When I refused he simply resorted to his wood chisel again. I realized I would have to stand firm about the can opener or risk losing my authority over Tam and Richie.

Now Tam stood looking down at the beans. He cleared them up by opening the door and flicking them outside with his boot. Then he sat down again and watched me finish shaving, while Richie lay on his bunk and read *An Early Bath for Thompson*. When I was ready we went out.

The landlord of the Queen's Head seemed quite pleased to see us.

'Like my beer, do you, lads?' he boomed as we walked in.

'It's alright,' Richie managed to say.

The few people in the bar seemed to be roughly the same crowd as the night before. The girls weren't there but it was only early, so we sat in our corner and waited for the evening to pass. When Tam bought the second round of drinks the landlord decided it was time to find out about the strangers. He targeted Tam, who had just carried one full glass across to our table, and was now going back to the bar for the other two.

'So . . .' he said, looking hard at the beer flowing into the final glass. 'What are you lads busy with down here?'

'Fencing at Bowland,' replied Tam.

The landlord looked at him and smiled faintly.

'Sorry, what was that?' he said.

'Fencing at Bowland,' Tam said again. A few seconds passed. I could see from the landlord's face that he still hadn't caught it. The embarrassing moment was approaching when he would have to ask for a third time. Interestingly, none of the others standing round the bar seemed to have grasped what Tam was saying either, even though they were now all listening. It must have been something to do with Tam's accent. I'd got used to it, having spent so much time with him and Richie, but at this moment he might as well have been speaking another language. For his part, he wasn't helping matters by just repeating 'Fencing at Bowland' all the time. Tam wasn't making himself very clear, but then again, why should he? He hadn't come in the pub to spend the evening being interrogated. Yet here he was, standing at the bar, each hand gripping a pint glass, with all eyes on him. He wasn't finding any of this particularly easy.

The landlord tried again. 'No, sorry, still didn't get it.'

'We're fencing at Bowland!' said Tam, raising his voice, and at last they understood.

'Oh, you're doing some fencing along there, are you?' said our host.

There was a murmur. And then a different sort of silence fell on that bar room. It was only for a moment, little more than the minor register of something, but it was there alright. The locals seemed to draw back, ever so slightly. One of them was sitting on a stool by the bar, and at last he spoke.

'All the fencing round here is done by the Hall Brothers.'

That was all he said, but with those few words we became outsiders again. As the silence faded away, Tam came back across to me and Richie. He placed our drinks on the table and sat down with his back to the bar.

'What does he mean by that?' he said.

'Nothing,' I replied. 'Pay no attention to him.'

'Who the fuck are the Hall Brothers?'

'How do I know?' I said. 'Forget it.'

And for the time being, apparently, he did. We had a few more drinks and then, when it became obvious the women were not going to make an appearance, we left.

As we departed the landlord said, 'Good night.'

No one else did.

5

'Posting up today,' I said.

'Yep,' said Tam.

'You going to get out of bed then?'

'Nope.'

This was Tam's day. The day we were going to hammer a post into the ground every three yards for the entire length of the fence. Tam was the best at handling the post hammer and he knew it. Not getting up was his way of exploiting his position. Neither Richie nor I had got up either, but that wasn't the point. Tam was the most important member of the gang today, so he would have to be the last to get up. It was only right.

I let him bask in his moment of glory for a while longer. Then I swung my legs out of bed and said, 'Alright then, me and Rich will have to do it.'

This did the trick. Tam was out of bed in an instant saying, 'Oh no you fucking don't.' Which was how I got them out on the hill by eight o'clock in the morning. I wanted to get an early start on the fence because the previous day's hold-ups meant we hadn't really got much done. Donald would probably have estimated that we were already two-thirds of a day behind schedule. I wasn't sure about that, but we certainly had some catching up to do.

It was going to be hard work. Once the ground wire was tightened and our straight line established, we then had to hammer in all these pointed posts to form the main body of the fence. The process was simple. You stuck a steel spike in the ground to make a 'starter' hole, then one person held the post in position (point downwards) while the other hit it with the hammer. When it was into the ground the correct depth, and checked for alignment, you moved on to the next post. And the next one. And the one after that. Over and over again.

We started from the bottom of the hill and worked up, Tam and Richie putting the posts in while I kept them supplied with fresh ones. Tam's hammering technique had been perfected over the years since he began fencing. He used the 'full swing' method, which was the most efficient if done properly, but potentially disastrous if it went wrong. It depended on the fencer's ability to land the hammer head square on top of the post at every attempt. Tam had that ability. He could swing the post hammer at arm's length in a full circle and bring it down hard and accurate time after time. If he missed he was likely to split the post, break the hammer, or endanger Richie. Usually he didn't, and Richie seemed totally confident as he stood there holding the posts.

It was quite satisfying to see them working their way up that hill. At last I felt we were getting somewhere. Alright, so it was a bit of a slog carrying all those posts up the slope, especially as I had to make a longer journey each time, but that was all part of the game. Even when Tam and Richie stopped halfway up the hill for a fag it was OK with me. I paused to watch the familiar ritual in the distance. Tam lowered the post hammer to the ground, straightened up and spoke to Richie. Then Richie took something from his shirt pocket, handed it to Tam, and began wriggling about trying to fish into his jeans. Why he couldn't keep both items in his shirt pocket remained beyond me. His jeans were obviously far too tight for him, and it was a real struggle getting at that lighter. Eventually he succeeded, though, and they lit up and stood close together as smoke drifted away along the side of the hill. When I clambered towards them with another few posts on my shoulder, they started work again.

As further progress was made along the fence, I again became aware of how poorly sound carried. I would see the tiny, far-away figure of Tam swing the hammer, strike the post, and swing again, yet the 'clop' of the impact came to me about a second later. This had the odd effect of making Tam and Richie seem to be moving in a different world to me. As I said, it was a hard day. Eventually we reached the summit and began working down the other side of the hill. By the time we got back to the caravan that night we were all whacked. After we'd had our supper we stretched out on our bunks and dozed. Richie attempted to press on with *An Early Bath for Thompson*, but he soon nodded off. I closed my eyes.

Next thing I knew Tam was shaking me awake. It was dark in the caravan and there was panic in his voice. 'What time is it?'

Richie muttered something from his bunk and managed to light one of the lamps. It was half past ten!

'Fuck sake, the pub!' cried Tam, and next thing we were all screaming round in the caravan looking for our boots and rushing out into the night. The truck didn't start first time and there was a lot of shouting and cursing. Eventually we got going. We made the Queen's Head for last orders, thank God, or the evening would have been wasted altogether.

'Thought you'd forgotten us,' said the landlord as he pulled a double order of six pints.

'No, no,' said Tam.

We had two pints apiece, and they were the best beers any of us had ever had, ever. Even better, the two young women were lounging near the bar, watching the darts game in progress. Because we arrived late our usual table had already been taken, so instead Tam and Richie headed for a narrow wooden bench set into an alcove in the wall. They were still wearing their rubber workboots, and as they sat side by side holding their pints, they reminded me of gnomes on a shelf at a garden centre.

Next morning, as he selected a plate from the sink and scraped it clean, Richie made an announcement.

'I'll take the post hammer today,' he said.

Tam glanced at me and went and stood in the doorway, looking out of the caravan.

'Why's that then?' I said to Richie.

'I need the practice,' he replied.

This was well said. In spite of his other fencing skills, Richie had never quite mastered the post hammer. At best his aim was questionable. At worst . . . well, you have to remember the hammer had a cast iron head weighing several pounds. In the wrong hands it could be dangerous. Yesterday, Tam had only damaged one post out of all those he knocked in: a single mishit had caused a chip of wood to zing off sideways into the air. Furthermore, he had been going at such a good rate that there were only about twenty posts to do in that first fence. Richie wanted to hammer in these last few. He was quite determined, so we let him get on with it. Which meant that Tam had to hold the posts for him. I must admit I admired the way he didn't even flinch when Richie took his first swing of the day. I made a mental note to check how many spare posts we had, to replace the ones Richie was bound to split.

While they finished off that section I had some carpentry to do. The straining posts at each end of the fence had to be fitted with a support strut, and this was usually my job. Donald always specified that the timber be joined properly using a hammer and chisel. Some fencers just held the strut in position with six-inch nails but the company frowned on this practice. The strut was a good length of 4 × 4, set firm in the ground, and gave the high-tensile fence much of its strength and durability. I quite liked this job, and was always pleased when the join was neat and tidy.

Richie managed to complete the line of posts without damaging any or injuring Tam, so we were able to make good speed towards getting the rest of the wires towed out, tightened and fixed to complete the first fence.

That evening I decided to give Donald a ring to let him know how we were getting on.

'How are you getting on?' he asked.

'Not too bad,' I replied. 'Just about on schedule, I should think.'

'Good,' said Donald. 'And how are your two charges behaving?'

'They're being OK, actually,' I said. 'No problem at all.'

'Good,' said Donald again. 'We like all our gangs to be balanced.' There was a pause and then he said, 'By the way, there's something I've been meaning to ask you about Mr McCrindle.'

'Oh yes?'

'Are you sure you finished him off properly?'

'Er . . . how do you mean?'

'It's a simple enough question,' replied Donald. 'I just asked if you finished him off properly, that's all. Did you get the wires fully tightened, check the posts and so forth?'

'Oh,' I said. 'Er . . . yes. I'm sure the fence was all up to standard when we left.'

'And was it straight?'

'Perfectly.'

'I see.'

'Why's that then?'

'It's just that Mr McCrindle has failed to settle his account. I thought there may have been a problem of some kind.'

'Not as far as I know,' I said.

'Alright then,' said Donald. 'Keep in touch, won't you?'

'Righto. Bye.'

When I got back to the caravan Tam and Richie looked at me expectantly.

'What did Donald say?' asked Tam.

'Not much,' I replied. 'He said Mr McCrindle hasn't settled his account.'

'Oh fuck,' said Tam. 'I never thought of that.'

'Nor me,' I said.

'Did you ask him about our wages?' asked Richie.

'No, I forgot.'

'Oh, for fuck sake!' said Tam.

'Alright,' I snapped. 'I forgot, right? I'll go and ring him again.'

So I went back down to the phone box and rang again. Donald said the wages were ready, and I suggested he sent them to the general stores near the Queen's Head, which also acted as a sub-post office.

'There's a deduction to be made from Tam's money for a few days he was off last month,' he said.

'Have you told him?' I asked.

'Robert told him,' he replied. It was the first I'd heard of it. The company didn't have a regular pay day. It all depended where people were and how long jobs were expected to take. Money only turned up when we asked for it. As long, that is, as Donald agreed he owed us any.

The other thing about working for this company was that we didn't stop at weekends. We were expected to carry on working every day until the contract was complete. Unfortunately, Tam and Richie never seemed to get used to this idea, and when Friday came along, as it now had, they started to think in terms of 'going out'. Most of the day went OK, and we began to work on the cross-fence that would divide the hill the other way. As soon as we got back to the caravan that evening, however, Tam turned to me and said, 'Are you changing?'

I examined the backs of my hands. Then I peered closely in the mirror.

'Don't think so,' I replied.

Tam looked at me. 'You know what I mean,' he said. 'Are you changing to go out?'

'Spec so. Clean shirt . . . yeah.'

'Are you shaving?' he went on.

'I shave every day, don't I? Course I am.'

'So you're going to get ready?'

'Yes,' I said. 'When I've had my tea.'

Tam sighed and sat down on his bed. He looked over to Richie, who was standing by the sink. 'Are you getting ready, Rich?'

'Yep,' replied Richie. He had already taken a large saucepan from the sink and started cleaning it out. Then he put some water on the boil. While he waited he got his cowboy boots out of the cupboard and buffed them up with his spare underpants. When the pan boiled he poured the water into a bucket and topped it up with cold. Then he stuck his head in, added shampoo, and washed his hair. There was a lot of it. Both he and Tam seemed to be involved in some kind of competition to see who could grow their hair longest. I didn't know when they'd given up having it cut: probably the day they left school, whenever that was. It was all to do with their head-banger image. Now they were both 'long-haired', although Tam was clearly in the lead, which apparently dismayed Richie. His constant complaint against the world was that his hair had slowed down growing as soon as he stopped having it cut. He wanted his hair to be even longer to go with the electric guitar he couldn't play yet. If they'd lived in the dark ages they would have been Vikings. But they weren't. They were itinerant fencers. And on Friday nights, wherever they were, they washed their hair.

After washing, Richie towelled himself dry. Now came the

final part of the routine. First, he put on his denim jacket. Next he bent down, throwing his hair forward and then quickly straightening up again, at the same time flicking his head back, so that his hair fell over his shoulders like a lion's mane. He went to all this trouble because it was Friday night.

Now it was Tam's turn. He repeated the whole procedure, his head disappearing in a blur when he towelled himself dry at the end. I noticed for the first time that Tam had a tattoo on his forearm. It consisted of a diagonal flag and a scroll bearing the words, 'I'm a Scot'. However, the tattooist hadn't really left himself enough room, so the words actually read 'I mascot'.

When Tam and Richie had changed their jeans and put on their cowboy boots they considered themselves to be 'ready'. Now that the bucket was free, I got some water boiled and began to have a shave. There was a mirror halfway up the door of the caravan wardrobe, and every time I looked in it to see how the shave was going I could see Tam sitting on his bunk, watching, and waiting.

'I can't shave any faster,' I said.

'I don't know why you bother,' he remarked.

Richie had picked up his copy of *An Early Bath for Thompson* by A. D. Young, and started reading again.

'What's that about then?' I asked.

'Don't know,' he replied. 'I haven't finished it yet.'

It was half past seven before I was ready to leave.

'If we're going to be drinking all night Rich'll have to drive,' I said.

'Alright,' said Richie, without further comment, and we set off for a wonderful evening at the Queen's Head.

I was interested to see if Tam and Richie would do anything

different tonight, considering all the trouble they'd just gone to with their hair and so on. I was surprised, therefore, when they went and sat at our usual table in the corner. I'd have thought it would be better to hang round the bar if they wanted to get anywhere with the two women who had been ignoring them all week. Instead their technique was to sit behind their pints and wait to see what happened. All night if necessary. When we got there at ten to eight there was hardly anybody in, so the wait was going to be a long one. The place did eventually fill up, though, and even had a weekend feel to it. I suspected I would be incapable of drinking the amount Tam and Richie planned to, so I dropped out after the first three rounds and went and put my name up for the darts knockout. It would make a change, and I could talk to other people. Furthermore, there was a higher ratio of women in this part of the pub. I'd just positioned myself by the bar when the landlord, who had glanced our way a couple of times during the evening, suddenly turned to me and said, 'How's the fencing going?'

There was something odd about this. Over the last few days he'd ceased questioning us about 'what we were getting up to' and started treating us like normal customers. Now, however, he seemed to have reverted to his previous ways. Except that there was a slight difference in his tone. It was almost as if the question was directed to me, but actually meant for somebody else's ears. If any heads turned as he spoke, I didn't notice. I just said something like 'Not too bad really' and carried on watching the darts game. After a while I glanced over towards Tam and Richie, wondering if they'd heard the brief conversation. It appeared they hadn't, for they were now isolated in their corner, cut off from the central attraction, namely the darts knockout, by a knot of standing drinkers. Tam and Richie just stayed there with their pints. I also noted that the two regular women who had been the original attraction to this pub finally turned up with men who were obviously their husbands. I got through the first round of the darts knockout OK, but failed to survive the second. The victor and I both said 'bad luck' and 'well done' at the same time, shook hands (each attempting to crush the other's bones), and then I bought him the obligatory pint.

I made my way back through the throng to Tam and Richie.

'You got beat then,' said Tam.

'Yes, thanks,' I replied.

Judging by all the empty glasses on the table they'd had a good night. They were both yawning a lot, which I regarded as an encouraging sign, because the sooner I could get them home, the better would be the chance of getting them up to work in the morning. There was still time for another drink before closing, however, and so, inevitably, we had one.

'This is shite,' said Tam. 'There's no women.' This wasn't in fact the case. There were quite a few women in the pub this evening. I knew what he meant though.

'We'll have to go into town tomorrow night,' he added.

'Right,' I said. 'I'll look forward to that.'

Eventually we were turfed out into the night. I handed Richie the keys to the truck and tried not to think too hard about the journey home. He didn't seem to have any trouble getting out of the car park, so I left him to it. Tam had fallen silent just before we left the pub, but now, as we got going, he spoke at last.

'What did the landlord say to you?'

'When?'

'Up at the bar, you were talking to him during the darts.'

'Oh nothing,' I said. 'Nothing. He just asked how the fencing was going, that's all.'

'Why did he want to know that?' he asked.

'Dunno,' I replied.

'You do really,' said Tam.

'No I don't.'

'You do.'

'Look,' I said. 'I don't know what you're talking about.'

'There were some guys staring at us,' said Richie.

'Were there?' I said. 'I didn't notice.'

'Hall Brothers,' said Tam.

'What?'

'That's who it was.'

'How do you know that?' I asked.

'I just do that's all.'

'But it could have been anybody.'

Tam turned and looked at me. 'Why were they staring at us then?'

'I don't know.'

'Because they've heard we're here!' And with that he put his arm out through the open window and banged on the cab roof with his fist. Richie, who was driving quite well for someone containing almost a gallon of beer, took no notice of the disturbance and drove us home.

By the time we got back Tam had stopped going on about the Hall Brothers and slumped into oblivion. I was hoping this would be him out for the rest of the night, but when we were manhandling him into the caravan he came round and insisted on having a fag. He also lit the portable gas fire. The weather had been getting chilly over the last week and there was nothing unusual about doing this. The problem was that he had a habit of sitting right up close to the fire and then dozing off. A couple of times already he'd come close to catching alight, and I'd had to shout to wake him up. Now he was guarding the fire jealously and could not be persuaded to turn it off until he was warm.

Richie said, 'Might as well leave him,' and went to bed. Eventually I did the same, hoping Tam wouldn't burn us all to death.

In the middle of the night there was a crash. I came awake aware that Tam's end of the caravan was glowing red from the firelight. Tam himself was now on the floor between his bed and the sink. I got up and turned the gas off. Then, at last, we all slept.

When I woke up next morning I realized that, like Tam and Richie, I didn't like working on Saturdays much either. My head was throbbing from the drink. Worse, there was rain falling on the caravan roof. To people who work outside all day this is one of the most desolate sounds known. Rain can transform the most pleasant task into drudgery. The only reason we had managed to keep the job just about on schedule (more or less), was because the weather had stayed dry. Now we faced a muddy, soaking wet struggle from the moment we went out in the morning until the end of the day. And, of course, the squalor inside the caravan would reach new depths, with wet clothing hanging everywhere and mud on the floor. All we had to dry us off was the gas fire. I lay on my bed thinking about this and wondering how I was going to motivate Tam and Richie to get up.

Nevertheless, if we were ever going to get away from Upper Bowland the job was going to have to be completed, sooner or later. We would just have to get on with it. I got up and managed some breakfast, hoping to stir Tam and Richie into life. There was little sign of movement, so I decided to go and collect our wages from the sub-post office, where they should have arrived by now. I got back about quarter to ten and found them sitting on their bunks, smoking, and apparently ready for work. The settling of Tam's debts turned out to be less difficult than I had expected. Inside the registered letter (addressed to me) were three separate pay packets. Figures were written on the outsides, in Donald's handwriting, explaining the various deductions. Tam's packet was noticeably thinner than mine or even Richie's.

We all opened up and checked the contents. Tam seemed to accept straight away that his would be less than ours. Richie, meanwhile, was folding his notes with an awkward gesture before putting them in his jeans pocket (at the back, not the one he kept his lighter in.)

Tam looked at me, grinned, and said, 'Fuck it . . . c'mon then, what am I due you?'

I told him and he counted out the sum.

After a dutiful pause Richie spoke, 'You're due me some too.'

'It's alright, Rich,' replied Tam. 'What was it again?'

'Just give me what you can,' said Richie.

'No, no, I'll pay in full,' Tam insisted.

'Er . . . OK, then.' And Richie told Tam the bad news.

'Fuck me, I'm back where I started,' said Tam, handing Richie his entire wedge apart from some coins.

'Never mind. I'll lend you some until next week,' promised Richie. And he did, there and then, on the spot.

A thought then occurred to Tam. 'What about your guitar instalments, Rich?'

'It came out of my mother's catalogue,' replied Richie. 'She's going to pay them till I get back.'

So that was alright.

When they had their breakfast Tam asked me if he could possibly have a lend of my can opener for their beans.

Yes, I said, just this once he could.

Eventually, on that dismal autumn Saturday, we dragged our-selves into the rain to do some work. I was lucky in that at least I had a full set of waterproofs. Richie had just the top half of his, but didn't seem the slightest bit bothered about his jeans getting soaked, and probably wouldn't have worn the water-proof bottoms even if he had had them. That just left Tam, who only had his leather jacket. He'd bought this new sometime in the summer, and hadn't originally intended to work in it. However, at some stage he had caught sight of a friend's jacket that had seen a few seasons on a motorcycle, and decided that his own didn't look worn enough. It was too crisp and shiny for his liking. So he started 'wearing it in' at work, deliberately scuffing it against things, and generally treating it roughly. As a result, now that the autumn rains were here, it was already showing signs of falling to pieces. As a waterproof it was next to useless. Still, he persevered with it for the time being as he had nothing else.

We continued work on the cross fence as best we could while the rain showed no sign of letting up. By mid-afternoon, however, discussions about posts and wire began to be interrupted by talk of 'tonight', even though I for one was still feeling the after-effects of the night before. Richie had taken over the post hammer again, and this time I was his assistant while Tam did the fetching and carrying. I asked Richie how his hangover was.

He looked at me. 'What hangover?'

'Haven't you got one then?' I said. I could tell by his expression that he had no idea what I was talking about, so I abandoned the conversation.

On one of Tam's trips he seemed to take longer than usual to return, and we began to wonder what had happened to him. Finally, coming up the slope carrying a load of posts, we spotted what appeared to be a fertilizer sack on legs. It laid the posts out along the fence, ignoring us completely, and retreated down the hill again. Shortly afterwards the figure returned with another load. By this time Richie and I were having difficulty concentrating on what we were doing. Tam had evidently got fed up with being soaked through and decided to make himself a 'waterproof' out of a heavy duty plastic fertilizer sack he'd found under a seat in the truck. He'd cut holes for his arms and head, while his legs protruded out of the open end. He had made the neck hole as small as possible to prevent water getting in, and then forced his head through without bothering to untrap his hair, so that it resembled a medieval helmet.

In this guise Tam marched up to where me and Richie stood looking.

'Something funny?' he said.

'No, no,' replied Richie.

'Well get on with your work then,' he snapped.

We obeyed, and he set off down the hill again. Shortly after this incident Richie lost control of the post hammer during a particularly violent swing, and I decided it was time to swap jobs.

And so we slogged on, spending our Saturday afternoon working on a drenched hillside, until we had had enough. Then we followed the line of posts to the bottom of the hill, and walked round to where the truck was waiting. The three of us sat in the cab for a few minutes while Tam and Richie had their first 'dry' fag for several hours, and then I started the engine and we trundled slowly back down the track towards the caravan. We were just about to turn into the farmyard when our eyes fell on something that hadn't been there this morning. Along the side of the track, from the farmyard to the front gate, someone had built a brand new fence. It was strong and straight, and the wires gleamed in the half light of dusk.

'Where the fuck did that come from?' said Richie.

Tam stamped his feet. 'The Hall Brothers have been here!' he announced.

'You don't know that for sure,' I replied, but I suspected he was right.

'Bet it was them,' he said. 'Let's have a look.'

We got out of the truck and examined the mystery fence. It was a smart, classy job. The style was different to ours: they'd used mild steel netting instead of high-tensile wires. Also, the posts were round in cross-section, whereas we always worked with square ones. But we could not fault the fence itself. It was perfectly straight, the wire was tight, and the posts were firm in the ground.

'Look at this,' said Richie.

He had come across a silver tag attached to one of the posts, indented with some lettering: HALL BROS.

So now we knew.

6

'Told you it was them!' shouted Tam. He was practically dancing around.

'There must be four of them,' said Richie.

Yes, I thought, there must indeed be four of them. How else could they have got the job done so quickly? Not only had they built this new fence, but they had also demolished the old ruined one that was there beforehand, and taken away all the scrap timber and wire. What was most disconcerting though, was that they had been here while we'd been working away up on that hill, and we had never even known. All that rain had meant the cloudbase was very low and we'd been more or less cut off from the rest of the world all day. Furthermore, this was the first time we hadn't come down off the hill for lunch. Usually we trooped back at midday for a rest, even though it went against Donald's Code of Practice (he said it was an inefficient waste of time). Today, however, because we started late, we took sandwiches with us. (If you could call them sandwiches, that is. Richie made them. Pieces of bread separated by cheese would be a better description.) We'd loaded up the truck with enough posts and wire for a day's work, and hadn't returned since. That was, what? Seven hours. And now here was a shiny new fence, built out of the blue while our backs were turned. The confounded cheek of these people! The Hall Brothers had acted as if they owned the place. What if we'd come back and caught them at it? They must have known we were around: there was a huge stack of timber and stuff right nearby in the farmyard. And what was Mr Perkins doing hiring two sets of contractors to work on one farm? Playing the field? I suppose the Hall Brothers had as much right to be there as we did, but even so, it was three distracted fencers who sat brooding in the caravan that evening. It seemed to have affected Tam a great deal, and he was full of speculation.

'Do you think they get paid more, or less, than us because there's four of them?' he asked.

'I don't know,' I replied.

'Because if they divide the money up four ways there'll be less each, but they can get more done at a time, so there's more to divide.'

'We don't even know if there are four,' I said.

'Oh, it'll be four alright. Four brothers.'

'You certain about that?'

'They always come in fours,' he said. 'With a year between them.'

'It could be three brothers and their father,' I suggested.

'No,' he replied. 'That would be Hall and Sons.'

Now Richie joined in. 'How come Donald can afford to send us all the way down here and still make a profit, when people like the Hall Brothers are around?'

'It's all a question of scale,' I explained. 'We're doing a big project fencing off the whole of that hill. The Hall Brothers' fence is only a short little thing, isn't it?'

Nods of approval.

'They probably don't even know how to do high-tensile fencing,' I went on. 'We're supposed to be specialists, after all.'

This seemed to satisfy Tam and Richie. Following all that questioning, it was a relief when the conversation reverted to the usual talk of going out, and Tam asked me when I was getting ready. I decided it would be a good idea to avoid the Queen's Head tonight. Besides which, Tam and Richie had been making it clear they'd like to go back to that last town we passed through on the way down. Donald didn't really like us to go too far afield in the truck, but I thought, 'How will he know?'

Anyway, we could easily stick a couple of extra gallons of diesel in the truck to cover the mileage. So I pre-empted them and suggested going into town. As long as Richie drove. Again he showed not the slightest objection, so it was agreed. Tam had by now removed his fertilizer bag, so we put the pan on to boil and repeated last night's performance with the bucket, one after the other, until we were all ready to go out. As we left the farm we tried to splatter some mud on the Hall Brothers' new fence.

We found a few good pubs that night, but unfortunately Tam and Richie didn't have the patience to remain in any of them more than the length of time it took to drink one pint. On this occasion they forgot to mention that the beer was weak, even though it came from the same brewery as the Queen's Head. The whole population of the town seemed to be on the move. Just the same as any other English small town on a Saturday night. There were crowds of people herding from one pub to another like wildebeest in the rainy season. With us three following them. After a few hours in this town we almost knew our way round. We'd also found out that the 'big deal' here was a night club called Carmens (Saturdays and Wednesdays). There were flyers advertising it all over the place, and we also heard it mentioned in various pubs.

'That's where we'll go,' said Tam, as we sat in the Six Bells.

'Not tonight,' I said.

'Why not?' Tam and Richie both looked at me in disbelief.

''Cos we've got to work tomorrow,' I replied.

'Fuck work,' said Tam.

'We'll come Wednesday,' I heard myself say, and they accepted the offer. Shortly after that we managed to lose Richie. I'm not sure how it happened, but one minute he was trailing along behind me and Tam, then suddenly he was gone. I suspect he dodged up a side alley for a slash without saying anything, and it had taken longer than he expected to get mobile again, by which time he'd lost us. Tam was most agitated when we discovered that Richie was missing, and wanted to trace our steps back to every pub we'd visited during the evening. I pointed out that it would make just as much sense looking in all the pubs we hadn't tried yet. No, I argued, it would be better staying put in one pub until he found us. We tried this for a while, but Tam went to the doorway and looked out so many times that in the end I got fed up and agreed to go in search of Richie.

'Maybe he's gone to Carmens,' I suggested.

Tam looked at me. 'On his own?' he said.

I thought about this. 'No, I suppose not,' I conceded.

Eventually we found him sitting in the truck, on his own, in the dark.

'I've been here an hour,' he complained.

I had hoped that the reunion would have the necessary calming effect on Tam, but both he and Richie were so bothered at having lost all that valuable drinking time that I knew there would be no peace until we got to another pub. We just made it as normal drinking hours came to an end, in a pub that was obviously on the wildebeest circuit, judging by the press of excited bodies. Everybody in town, apparently, was going to Carmens. As usual Tam and Richie did nothing to make contact with any women in the vicinity and merely sat side by side on a bench holding their pints.

Before we could go home Tam insisted on getting fish and chips. By the time he'd queued and got served the beer had begun to affect his judgement, so he ordered all the extras and came out of the shop with enough chips for several men.

We stood outside on the pavement, swaying on that Saturday night in a bleak and windy small town street. Opposite the chippie was a parade of other shops, all with their shutters pulled down. The shop we all noticed was the one with the big sign across the front: HALL BROTHERS QUALITY MEATS.

'For fuck sake, they're fucking butchers as well!' yelled Tam, hurling his spare chips across the street.

Getting up for work on Sunday morning was even worse than Saturday. The rain had eased up into a drizzle, which meant never being sure whether it was worth wearing waterproofs or not. If you did wear them, you sweated so much that you still ended up wet through anyway. This was a problem only for me, of course. Richie's work jeans were still wet from yesterday because he'd forgotten to dry them over the gas fire. He went ahead and wore them all the same, and sat eating his cornflakes with steam slowly rising from his legs. Tam opted for the fertilizer bag again. We were sitting in the caravan trying not to think about going out in the wet. The carpet was damp since there was nowhere to put our boots outside the door, so we'd started wearing them inside as well. The fire was flickering because Tam had lit his fags off it so many times that the gauze was burnt through and didn't glow evenly. As soon as we went outside we knew we'd have water trickling down our necks for the rest of the day. And we still had the biggest part of the job ahead of us. The cross-fence would be finished sometime today, once we got all the wires pulled out and tightened up. After that we had to build a long fence encircling the foot of the hill, to close off the four quarters we'd made. There were also a number of gates to hang, so that stock could be moved between the different areas. I decided to complete the cross-fence, and then work our way round the foot of the hill, section by section.

It was about ten before we got going properly, which I suppose was not bad for a Sunday morning. But we all seemed to be running out of energy. I stood by the unwinder and watched it as Tam towed yet another wire up the hill. Slowly and sporadically it turned as he made his way up and over the summit. It stopped. Then it continued a few turns. Then it stopped again. I waited. I guessed that Tam must have met Richie, who was working back the other way fixing the previous wire onto the posts. I wondered how long I should give them to exchange greetings. After a minute I grabbed the wire and gave it a jerk. The unwinder started to turn again. Then it stopped. I came to the conclusion that they must be having a fag. It was at such times that I seriously considered taking up smoking myself, just to pass the time.

In this haphazard way we progressed into the afternoon, and started work on the long encircling fence.

Which is when Richie managed, inevitably I suppose, to break the post hammer. My fault again. I should have insisted Tam did all the post driving. After all, as I said before, he was best at it. Specialization would have been more efficient: Richie digging, Tam hammering, and me supervising (and doing joinery). But somehow Richie had got hold of the post hammer again, and begun to get over-confident. I watched in slow motion as he brought the shaft down full whack on top of a post, so that the head broke off with a loud crack.

'Fuck,' he said, but I think he was more concerned about what Tam would say than about the damage to the hammer itself. That was my problem. We still had quite a few posts to knock in along this section before it could be wired up. Now I was going to have to find Tam and Richie other things to do while I went and got the hammer repaired. This involved seeking out a joiner's shop (there wouldn't be one open until Monday), leaving the hammer for repair, and then going back for it. Yes, I know we should have had a spare hammer with us, but you can't cover every contingency. Mending it ourselves was out of the question. The shaft had to fit perfectly, and I'd seen for myself many times before the consequences of working with a badly repaired post hammer. No. The job had to be done by a proper joiner who knew what he was doing.

Just then Tam came walking along the fence line. He took one look at the broken hammer and said, 'Ha. Call yourself a fencer?'

'Don't look at me,' I replied.

Tam glanced at Richie, who was reaching for something in his shirt pocket, and said no more about it.

7

An air of gloom hung over our camp when we returned that evening. I could really have done without this. While the post hammer was broken we would have to spend all our time digging holes for straining posts. This meant Tam and Richie having to work separately, and I'd already found that they coped much better when they were in sight of each other. (Even though they stopped for a fag break every time their paths crossed.) There was the possibility of having them work two-to-a-hole, but this was another practice which Donald had banned as inefficient. I could see there was a danger of work grinding to a halt unless I could get the post hammer repaired quickly. The weather wasn't helping matters either. It had now settled into what I call mizzle, and it was getting dark slightly earlier every day.

The thing I wasn't in the mood for was a discussion about what we were doing tonight, and Tam and Richie seemed to sense this. We sat in our three corners of the caravan, serenaded by Richie's stretching tape. All around me was encroaching squalor. Fortunately, much of it was hidden because the gas lights were so dim. Which is why, presumably, Richie had now abandoned *An Early Bath for Thompson*. Night after night he'd struggled with it, holding the book in all manner of positions under his lamp as he tried to have a read. Finally he gave up and shoved it back in the cupboard where it came from.

'What a fucking way to spend a Sunday night,' he said.

All this set the pattern for the next few days. Having given Tam and Richie some very specific tasks I went off the following morning in search of a joiner. All I had for guidance was Donald's photocopied road map. I was reluctant to go all the way back into town, so I set off in the other direction, hoping to come across somewhere suitable. Yes, not far along the road I would find a workshop, a busy efficient place where there would just happen to be a craftsman at a loose end who could fix the post hammer right away. Some hope. I drove for miles and found nothing. Eventually, after a bit of asking round, I was directed to some lock-up premises at one end of a converted bakery. Apparently they were let to a joiner who did most of his work elsewhere, but I might catch him if I was lucky. I wasn't. A sign on the door said he would be back later. I put a note through the letterbox saying I'd left a broken post hammer behind the dustbin and could he fix it please? I didn't have time to do anything else. On the way back I stopped at the general store to get some more food and stuff, and then returned to find Tam and Richie sitting in the caravan. They'd taken an early lunch.

'I'd have thought you'd want to get the job done as soon as possible so we can get home,' I said.

'Why should we do all the work while you go riding round in the truck?' said Tam.

'I had to get the post hammer fixed,' I pointed out.

'That's not work,' he replied.

The evenings, meanwhile, were spent deciding what time we would go to the pub. If we went too early, all our money would be spent on beer. While this was alright in itself, I for one wanted to have something left when we'd finished the job. Otherwise there was little point in going through all this hardship. Besides, Tam was deep in debt to Richie again, and couldn't really afford to go anywhere. On the other hand, there was no question of not going to the pub in the evening. If we didn't, we would go crazy with boredom. Things were quiet in the Queen's Head on weekdays, but it beat the caravan hands down for entertainment value.

On Tuesday night, by way of diversion, we went off to see if the post hammer was ready. In darkness we pulled up at the end of the converted bakery and Richie went over to the dustbin. In the glare of the headlights I witnessed a smile appear on his face as he raised a newly repaired hammer triumphantly above his head. Miracles can and do happen. We looked in the dustbin and felt inside the letterbox for an invoice, but there wasn't one.

And so another day passed and the long fence slowly grew around the foot of that hill. The next light at the end of the tunnel was Wednesday night at Carmens. I didn't mention it at all to Tam and Richie, but I could tell during Wednesday afternoon that expectations were beginning to rise again. Now that the post hammer was back in action, guarded closely by Tam, we were able to work in a tight three-man squad, section by section, along the fence. About four o'clock, as an incentive, I told Tam and Richie that we would finish the bit we were on and pack up for the night. I never saw them work so fast. Half an hour later they were back in the caravan with the pan boiling and the shampoo at the ready. Somehow it had been 'agreed' that I would drive tonight, so I resigned myself to an evening of Cokes. I wanted to shave first though, and was forced to go through the ritual under scrutiny from Tam and Richie, impatiently watching in the mirror.

At last I could delay no more, so we headed into town. As usual, we arrived far too early. There were no droves of people herding from pub to pub tonight. Like most other towns in England, the place had gone back to sleep for the week. We spent a long slow evening waiting for something to happen. It was only as closing time approached that people began to appear who were obviously going on somewhere else after-wards. That somewhere was Carmens Nightspot, to give it its full title. It turned out to be not as glamorous as it sounded. But it would do. At the top of some stairs we paid our money and they let us in. There was a bar at one side and a dance floor at the other. I was still getting my bearings in the gloom when a girl poked my arm and said, 'Got a light?'

'Er, no, sorry,' I replied. 'He has,' I added, pointing to Richie. I got his attention and he obliged by fishing his lighter out of his jeans. Apart from drinking bottled, instead of draught, beer, Tam and Richie did what they always did when I was out with them. They found somewhere to sit and watch what was going on, and stayed there. They probably thought they'd chosen a good place because it was near the bar and in sight of the dance floor. However, I got the feeling that if the club got any busier people would soon be tripping over their legs, which were sticking out from under a tiny table. There was already no room for me, so I positioned myself by a railing above the dance floor. During the next couple of hours I occasionally glanced over to where they sat. Except for taking turns to go to the bar and the gents, they never moved at all. Meanwhile, a small forest of club people grew around them, so that they slowly became lost from view, apart from the tops of their heads. The music was loud and the dance floor full. I watched for a while and then went to get myself another Coca-Cola. The bar was crowded, and as I stood there I felt the unmistakable shape of a female breast being pushed into my back. I half turned and saw the lighter girl standing behind me.

'Oh hello,' she said. 'Didn't see you there.'

Her name was Marina. She was a dentist's receptionist.

'You were in the Six Bells on Saturday, weren't you?' she said. 'With your two mates. Where are they?'

I nodded towards where I last saw Tam and Richie. 'Over there.'

'They look quite sweet,' she said.

This was the longest conversation we had. It was far too loud for much talking. When the music slowed down a bit we went onto the dance floor, and she let her feelings be known. This was one of those clubs where things came to an end pretty quickly. We were still on the dance floor when the music stopped and all the lights came on.

Something that had been lurking at the back of my mind now surged to the front. If I was going to go home with this girl, then I was going to have to drop Tam and Richie off first. Which meant she would have to sit on one of them in the truck. I put it off as long as possible, but finally, as the place began to empty, I casually strolled with Marina over to Tam and Richie's table.

'This is Tam and Richie,' I said. 'And this is Marina.'

They looked at us with glazed expressions. Tam stood up and swayed towards me.

'We going now then?' he said.

'Er . . . yes. See you outside in a minute,' I replied.

'C'mon, Rich.' Tam pulled Richie by his jacket and the two of them lurched out through the door.

'We'll have to drop them off at Upper Bowland,' I explained to Marina.

'OK then,' she said. I must admit she handled it all very well. She had to go to the ladies' room first, so I waited at the top of the stairs.

When she came out we walked up the road to where I'd parked the truck, but there was no sign of Tam and Richie. We spent a pleasant fifteen minutes sitting in the cab, waiting for them to show up. I wondered where they'd gone. Tam and Richie had been drinking since eight o'clock and it was getting late. A public clock chimed twice. We waited a bit longer.

And then, from somewhere in the middle of this now silent town, we heard a faint roar in the night. 'C'mon, English bastards!'

I started the engine and took the girl home.

8

Marina lived in a small flat above a shoe shop.

'Very nice,' I said, as we went in.

'It's only temporary,' she replied.

She was supposed to be making coffee, but somehow we never got round to it. Not long afterwards we entered the bedroom, where I noticed there were two single beds, each with a cabinet covered in women's things.

'Whose is that?' I asked, pointing to the extra bed.

'My flatmate's,' said Marina. 'She's staying at a friend's tonight.'

'That's handy,' I remarked.

'Yes,' she said, 'I suppose it is.'

I looked at her and realized that underneath her clothes she was completely naked. A few minutes later we lay quietly on the bed, and it felt as if I was alone with this girl on a remote and distant planet.

Then I remembered Tam and Richie.

'Not quite alone,' I heard myself say.

'Pardon?' she said.

'Sorry, nothing,' I answered, but the spell was broken. There wasn't much room in the bed and I hardly got any sleep.

In the morning Marina had to go to work and there was no breakfast. As we parted she said, 'I'm not a fence post, you know.'

I wasn't sure what she meant by that.

I went and bought some doughnuts in a cake shop. I had no idea where Tam and Richie could have got to, and wasn't sure what to do. I was reluctant to phone up Donald and tell him I'd lost them. Somehow I expected to see them at any minute, still wandering around the streets, possibly looking for me, but more likely waiting for the pubs to open again. I patrolled the town for a while, but they were nowhere to be seen. In deep thought I drove back to Upper Bowland. I dismissed the idea that Tam and Richie might have found their own way there. They had shown no interest in local geography since their arrival in England, and as far as I knew had hardly any money left. I was therefore surprised to find them both asleep in the caravan, fully clothed, Richie on his bed and Tam on mine. They stirred as I went inside, but I didn't wake them. For some reason I felt slightly indebted to them, and as soon as I saw them lying there asleep I decided to give them the day off.

I made myself some eggs for breakfast and after a while they woke.

'Morning,' I said.

'Do you have to say that every day?' replied Tam.

'What?' I asked.

'Mor-ning,' he said, in a sing-song sort of voice.

'It's fucking sarcastic, isn't it,' added Richie.

'Sorry,' I said.

They didn't seem very grateful when I said they could have the day off. I thought they would appreciate the gesture. I also hoped that they might get bored after a while and get round to cleaning up the mess in the caravan, or even decide to come and do some work on the fence after all. In the event they did none of these things. They just stayed in the caravan all day long, smoking, and waiting for me to come back so we could go out again.

In the meantime I spent the day working on my own, putting a couple of straining posts in the ground, and doing a bit of joinery. Around mid-afternoon I decided to walk over the hill, checking the two cross-fences, measuring them, and making sure we hadn't forgotten to do anything.

It was then that I found we had a visitor. I was just testing the wire tension near the top of the hill when I saw a man coming along the fence from the other end. For a moment I thought Mr Perkins had come to have a look, but I soon realized that this was someone altogether different. I'd only seen Mr Perkins in the darkness, but I knew this wasn't him. The visitor was a very big man in a rustic suit, and reminded me of a large pig. He appeared to be giving the fence a thorough examination as he walked along, tugging on the occasional wire and pushing the posts to see if they moved. When he got to the point where the two fences crossed he stopped. There were no gates up here because there was no need for any. All the gates were to be positioned at points around the foot of the hill, so his way was effectively barred. I registered the exact moment he noticed me as he looked left and then right, but he failed to give any acknowledgement. It was as if I was a mere fixture or fitting. He just carried on studying the details of the fence.

However, my presence was enough to prevent him from attempting to climb over, which I think he would have done if I hadn't been there. Instead, he stayed where he was, and ignored me as I approached. At last I stood directly opposite him at the other side of the fence. Only then did he look at me.

'Keeping busy?' he said.

'Just about,' I replied.

'That's good.' He turned sideways and stared out across the hillside. I waited. Then he looked at the sky.

'Met Perkins?' he asked.

'Only once,' I said.

'Don't talk to me about Perkins.'

In the awkward silence that followed he again began to examine the fence, frowning with preoccupation and glancing at me from time to time. Finally, he cast his eye along the line of posts.

'Exemplary,' he remarked, and began stalking off down the hill.

'And you're Mr . . . ?' I called after him.

'Hall,' he said over his shoulder. 'John Hall.'

I stood by the fence absorbing this information. At last I had come face to face with one of the Hall Brothers, but I still had no idea why he was so interested in our fence. It struck me that he didn't really look like a fencer at all. He was certainly a heavily built man, but a lot of it was fat. Somehow I just couldn't picture him digging post holes or swinging the post hammer. I wondered what the other brothers were like. Maybe it was them who built the fences and he was the brains behind the organization. Perhaps his brothers were big too, but more solid. Like barn doors. I realized that I was beginning to speculate like Tam, so I put Mr Hall out of my mind and carried on with my work. The weather had dried up, but was beginning to turn cool, and as dusk came a chilly breeze started to blow across the hillside. Finally I made my way back to the caravan.

When I'd gone down for my lunch Tam and Richie had been lolling about on their beds, passing the time doing nothing. Now, however, they sat looking out of the window, evidently awaiting my return. They'd even gone to the trouble of putting the kettle on.

As soon as I went into the caravan Richie said, 'There was a guy snooping round here this afternoon.'

'Was there?' I said, pretending not to be very interested.

'Big, fat fucker,' added Tam.

When I showed no reaction, Richie stood up and pulled a note out of his back pocket. 'He left this for you.'

The note was folded into four. I opened it and read 'See you here at eight o'clock.' It was signed J. Hall.

I glanced at Tam and Richie. They were both staring hard at me. It was obvious they must have read the note, but I said nothing and folded it up again. At last Tam could contain himself no longer. He leapt to his feet and shouted at the top of his voice, 'They're coming to get us!'

In doing so he somehow managed to smash the gas lamp at his end of the caravan, so that bits of glass flew everywhere, including into the waiting teapot.

'Alright, alright,' I said. 'We don't know what they want, do we?'

'Don't be a cunt,' said Richie. 'You know why they're coming.'

Tam stuck his face in mine. 'YAAAAAAAAAAAAAH!!' he cried. 'YAAAAAAAAH!' After he'd calmed down a bit I got him to clear up the glass and I had my tea. Then we began to wait for eight o'clock. I had been planning to go down to the phone box this evening to give Donald a progress report, but decided under the circumstances that it was better to defer the call for the time being. At half past seven I put some water on to have a shave. I didn't see why I should change my arrangements just because someone said they were coming at eight o'clock. As usual Tam and Richie watched the whole process. At ten to eight there was nothing left to do but sit and wait. Eight o'clock finally came and nothing happened. At ten past, however, some headlights swung up the track from the road. All three of us had our boots on, so we stepped out of the caravan into the yard. A moment later a large car appeared and drove up to where we stood.

Mr Hall was already speaking as he opened the door and got out.

'Right,' he announced. 'I want you to do some fencing for me. When can you start?'

In the dim light cast from the caravan I noticed that the rustic suit had gone and he was now wearing a white coat. The sort worn by butchers. It took me a second to register what he had said.

'We can't,' I replied. 'We're already working for a company.'

Mr Hall then did what he had done on the hill in the afternoon, and completely ignored me.

'There's eight hundred yards to do by Monday, so the sooner you start the better,' he said. 'How much gold will you want for doing that?'

He thrust his hands in his coat pocket, looked at the ground and waited. I found myself looking at the ground as well.

'So?' he said.

I glanced up at him, thinking he would still be looking at the ground. Instead his eyes were fixed on me.

'We're working for somebody else,' I said.

At this moment I sensed that Tam wanted to say something, but he and Richie had both slipped into their usual silent routine, so it was all left to me.

'You'll have to do it as a foreigner,' said Mr Hall. 'Come on, we'll go for a drink.' He opened the back door of his car and indicated that the three of us should get in. Then he drove us to the Queen's Head. On the way out we rolled slowly past the new HALL BROS. fence, which he silently scrutinized from behind the wheel, post by post.

As we walked into the pub, the landlord was slouching over the bar reading a newspaper. The moment he saw Mr Hall he practically stood to attention. 'Evening, John,' he boomed. Likewise, several drinkers around the bar greeted Mr Hall by his first name, but in the same subservient way, as if doing so conferred some sort of honour on them. Meanwhile, Tam, Richie and myself were treated as if we were new disciples. One of the locals winked at us and tapped his nose significantly, after first glancing at Mr Hall to make sure he wasn't looking.

'Give these lads a pint apiece and rustle them up some grubbage,' ordered Mr Hall.

He turned to us. 'You haven't eaten, have you?'

We had, but we all shook our heads.

He led us over to our usual table in the corner and we sat down. The landlord bustled over with a tray bearing our drinks. Mr Hall, I noticed, was drinking orange squash.

'Everything alright, John?' said the landlord. I was surprised he didn't say Sir, or even King, John.

John Hall ignored him and sipped his squash. 'Bloody stuff,' he said.

The landlord retreated, and then there was an expectant silence, which I finally broke. 'Is that a butcher's coat?' I said.

'Yes it is,' he replied. 'We're butchers. Should have stayed that way as well.'

We nodded but said nothing, and he went on.

'Started as butchers and then we bought some land and raised our own beasts. Then we had too many beasts and had to buy more land and replace the fences. That's how we got into fencing, but we've taken on too much work.'

'Who does the fencing?' I asked.

'My brother,' he replied.

'What, on his own?'

Tam and Richie, who had been silently studying their pints, both looked up at Mr Hall.

'Course not,' he said. 'Got some lads in to do it, but they've gone off.'

The landlord came back, this time carrying three plates of steak and kidney pie.

'I've given them some of your specials, John,' he said.

'Yes, yes, alright,' snapped Mr Hall, and again the landlord retreated.

As we ate John Hall produced a large folded plan from his coat pocket and opened it on the table. I could see that it was a map of Mr Perkins's farm and the hill we were working on.

He chose a point on the hill and put his finger on it.

'This is where we stood,' he said. He took out a pencil and

wrote WE STOOD on the map. Then he swept his hand across the bottom corner.

'This land here's ours,' he said. 'And it needs a new boundary fence. Perkins says it's our responsibility. The lads did some the other day, but they've gone off now.'

He didn't explain why or where they'd gone. He folded the map and pushed it towards me.

'You'll have to do the rest,' he said.

'Does Mr Perkins know you've approached us?' I asked.

'None of his business,' he replied.

I made one more attempt to hold out. 'Our boss won't like it,' I said.

He raised his voice. 'What's the matter with you? You're getting beer, grubbage and cash in hand. What more could you want?'

A couple of people at the bar were now looking in our direction.

I turned to Tam and Richie. 'Alright?'

They both nodded.

'Alright then,' I said to Mr Hall. He grunted and ordered more drinks. So there I was, committed. Which meant we were going to be at Upper Bowland for even longer. I don't think Tam and Richie had thought about this part of the equation. All they were interested in was the cash Mr Hall was going to pay us. As soon as he'd dropped us off at the caravan they began talking as if we were going to land a windfall. They seemed to forget all the extra work we would have to do. Mr Hall was their benefactor, and after all the beer he'd bought them they would not have a word spoken against him.

'We'll be in trouble if Donald finds out,' I said.

'We won't tell him, will we?' replied Tam.

I supposed not. I had to admit the idea of a bit of extra cash in hand was attractive, and if we got stuck in over the weekend we could easily get the work done by Monday.

Even so, I had the usual trouble dragging them out of bed the following morning. We were supposed to meet Mr Hall's brother David along the road at eight o'clock. We needed to get going before that though because the first thing we had to do was go up onto the hill and get our tools. We got to the roadside meeting place on time, and the brother turned up at ten past eight in a small flatbed lorry loaded with posts and wire. He was like a slightly deflated version of John Hall, only much more cheerful. In fact he seemed to have a constant line of banter.

'Hoo hoo!' he chimed through the cab window as he pulled up. 'Beer and skittles, eh lads? Ha ha!'

Tam and Richie took to him instantly, even though he declined the offer of a fag. Personally I thought he went on a bit too much. He kept making jokes about fencing which involved parrying with an imaginary sword and shouting *en garde* every few minutes. As far as our sort of fencing was concerned, I was unable to picture him swinging a post hammer or digging holes. However, he was a pleasant enough bloke, and obliged us by driving the lorry slowly along the proposed fence line while Tam and Richie threw the posts off the back.

The fence itself looked like a straightforward enough piece of work. After David Hall had gone Tam went marching about chanting 'Easy! Easy!' at the top of his voice. He was right, it was easy. But it was also going to be a boring slog. We were used to building fences over sloping land and difficult terrain.

That was our speciality after all. This fence, though, just went on and on along the edge of the Hall Brothers' land. It was all flat. There were also a hell of a lot of posts to put in. Unlike the high-tensile fence we were building on the hill, this was a conventional wire-netting job. The posts had to be two yards apart to support the net, which meant there were four hundred of them! By the middle of the afternoon, knocking in post after post after post, the monotony was getting to us. Tam had taken to counting how many posts were already in, and how many were left to do. This seemed to make matters worse.

'That's one hundred and forty seven,' he would announce, as another post was completed. 'Three more and it's a hundred and fifty.'

And so on. I began to wonder if all this was really worth it. The only advantage I could see was that Tam would be solvent again when Mr Hall paid us on Monday. Which would take the pressure off me to keep providing subs, especially as now Richie was running short too, having himself lent so much to Tam. It suddenly struck me that we were expecting to get paid as soon as we finished the work. What if Mr Hall held out for a while before settling up? We hadn't thought of that. I didn't mention the possibility to Tam and Richie in case it affected their workrate. I didn't want them to lose their momentum so that we ended up with two uncompleted jobs on our hands. My suspicions deepened that evening when David Hall came by with several pounds of sausages for us. I hoped the Hall Brothers were not going to try to fob us off by paying us in kind. Tam and Richie, on the other hand, saw the sausages as a bonus, and when we got back to the caravan they began frying them for our tea. 'Did you have to cook the whole lot?'

I said, as Tam attended to a fully laden frying pan. He was stabbing the sausages one by one with a fork.

'Yah,' he said. 'There's plenty more where these came from.'

'You think so?'

'I know so. From now on it's gonna be beer and skittles for us.'

'You mean cakes and ale.'

Tam looked at me. 'I know what I fucking mean.'

It took us a while to recover from all those sausages, and the hard day's work, but we eventually made it to the Queen's Head, where the landlord stood us our first round of drinks and told us to call him Ron. It was as if our dealings with Mr Hall had bestowed on us some sort of special status. During the evening Tam and Richie were invited to make up the pub darts team, despite their having shown no previous interest in the game. I was left out, but I tried not to take this as a personal snub. When Tam rolled up his sleeves to play, I again looked at the words 'I mascot' tattooed on his arm. It came as no surprise that Tam's throwing was fairly accurate, while Richie's shots tended to be consistently wayward. It was a passable evening, but when we got home that night it was obvious that I was now the only one with any money left. And it was Saturday tomorrow.

I was wondering why Richie was taking such a long time to come back. This seemed to happen whenever I sent him off to do something. He was supposed to be working alone at the other end of Mr Hall's fence, stapling the wire netting onto the new line of posts, and should have finished the job ages ago. Eventually, I walked back to see what was going on, and found him knocking the staples in with a large stone. I observed this primitive scene for a moment, and then asked him where his hammer was.

He nodded towards the hill. 'Up there.'

'But we went up yesterday morning to get our tools,' I said.

'I didn't think I needed my hammer,' he replied.

'Why not?'

'Just didn't.' He stood holding the stone.

'Why didn't you borrow Tam's?' I asked.

'He lost his last week. He's been using mine ever since.'

'He lost his hammer?'

'Yep.'

I took my own hammer from my belt and handed it to Richie.

'Well, why didn't you ask me?' I said.

'I didn't think you'd lend me yours. You wouldn't let us borrow your can opener, would you?'

'That was different.'

In silence I walked back to where Tam was getting the next straining post dug in. He began working extra hard as I approached, and only stopped when I got right up to him.

'Any chance of a sub tonight?' he said, straightening up.

'How much?' I asked.

'Well, the usual, I suppose,' he replied.

'It's a loan, not a sub,' I said.

Tam nodded. 'That's OK.'

I was not particularly flush myself by now. Donald was being a bit tardy about getting the wages sent down. Still, I was doing all the business with Mr Hall, so as long as he paid up on time, I'd be able to recover my money from Tam. I therefore agreed to a further loan.

'Rich needs some as well,' he said.

'Have you lost your hammer?' I asked, changing the subject.

'How did you know that?' he said.

'I just guessed,' I replied.

There was a pause.

'Are you going to give Rich a sub then?' he asked.

'Yeah, I suppose so.'

'Right, I'll go and tell him.' Next thing he was marching off along the fence line. I watched as Tam and Richie met up in the distance. There was a moment's delay, and then Richie reached for something in his shirt pocket. A few seconds later a small cloud of smoke appeared above their heads.

Each section of Mr Hall's fence had to be finished off with a strand of barbed wire running along the top. Barbed wire was one of the worst materials I ever had to work with. It had a habit of curling off in its own direction if unrestrained, or of attaching itself to you like a spiky snake when you were trying to get it sorted out. It came in heavy coils that wouldn't fit on the unwinder. Instead they had to be rolled out along the ground before the wire could be tightened and fastened. All very awkward. The first section of netting was complete, so I asked Tam to start rolling out some barb. He selected a coil and began to examine it closely, looking for the end of the wire. When I looked across a minute later he was still there, peering intently at the coil and slowly turning it round. I stopped what I was doing and watched him. At last he called me over.

'This roll hasn't got an end,' he announced.

'It must have,' I replied.

'Show me then.' He stood back and I took over the examination. Somewhere, hidden in all those multiple layers of wire,
had to be an end. After several minutes I had to admit that I
couldn't find it either. This was ridiculous. All of us had started
off any number of rolls of barbed wire, and had never had this
trouble before. Yet this particular one was, apparently, without
an end. Just then Richie came walking along the fence.

'Got a fag, Rich?' said Tam.

'Not now!' I snapped. 'Let's get this coil started first.'

Richie said he would have a go, and began to study the coil.
When he looked up from the puzzle and saw me and Tam
watching him intently he got agitated and said he couldn't do
it with us there. So we went off and worked on the next section.
After a few minutes we saw Richie rolling the coil out along
the fence line.

'You found it then?' I said.

'Of course,' he replied. 'Just needed a bit of perseverance,
that's all.'

Later that afternoon we came to a part of the boundary that
ran along a dense hedgerow. Tam and Richie were supposed
to have laid all the pointed posts out when they were throwing
them off the back of David Hall's lorry, but there was no sign
of any along this section. I asked them where they were.

'They're over the other side of the hedge,' said Richie.

'What are they doing there?' I asked.

'We didn't know which side the fence was going.'

'Well, why didn't you ask?'

He shrugged. 'Couldn't be bothered.'

I sent them off to bring the posts back round to this side. In the meantime I began to set out a straight line for us to work along.

Tam and Richie had only been gone a few minutes when an irate voice spoke behind me.

'What's going on?'

9

I turned towards the newcomer. 'Pardon?'

'I said what's going on?' The man's face, I noticed, was pink. His voice seemed familiar.

'Mr Perkins?'

'You know it's Mr Perkins!' He appeared to be very angry about something.

'Anything wrong?' I asked.

'Don't give me that!' he said. 'You're supposed to be working on my hill! I've just been up there and you've abandoned the job! It's like the Retreat from Moscow!'

'Well,' I said. 'It's not quite like that.'

'Don't tell me what it's not quite like!!' he bellowed, taking a step towards me.

At that moment a post came flying over the hedge and struck him on the back of the head. He made a further step forward and fell into my arms. At the same time another post, and then another, came hurtling over.

'Who threw that?' I shouted.

'Me, Rich!' came the reply.

'Well, you'd better stop! You've just hit Mr Perkins!'

The posts stopped coming over. I looked at Mr Perkins. He'd

gone very quiet. In fact, he wasn't just quiet, he was dead. I leaned him upright against the hedge, and he sank slowly back into the foliage. After a while Tam and Richie appeared, both carrying pointed posts on their shoulders.

'We thought it would be quicker to throw them over,' said Tam.

'It probably is,' I replied. 'But you should be more careful. Look what Rich's done.'

Neither Tam nor Richie seemed to have noticed Mr Perkins standing in the hedgerow. When I nodded towards him they put down their posts and had a closer look.

'I didn't mean to do that,' said Richie.

'I know you didn't,' I said.

'What was he doing here?'

'He'd come to complain about something.'

All four of us stood there for a few moments.

'What are we going to do with him?' asked Tam.

'We'll have to bury him, I suppose.'

'But on his own land, not here,' suggested Richie.

'Good point,' I replied. 'We could put him under one of the new gateposts by the hill.' (Strictly speaking, we weren't quite ready to hang any gates yet, but under the circumstances it was probably worth bringing the work forward.)

'I could collect my hammer at the same time,' said Richie.

We decided to sit Mr Perkins in the front of the truck between me and Richie, with Tam riding in the back. However, when we came to move him we found he wouldn't bend into the correct position. So we put him in the back and drove him round to the bottom of the hill. All the proposed gateways had been marked out when Donald originally surveyed the job, so we chose the one we thought would be the most suitable for Mr Perkins and dug the post holes. After a short discussion we all agreed it was best to put him under the slamming post, rather than the hanging post, although none of us could come up with a particular reason why this should be so. Mr Perkins's gateway looked quite nice when it was finished, even though it wouldn't actually lead anywhere until the surrounding fences were complete.

As we put the gear back in the truck a thought occurred to me.

'He was dead, wasn't he?'

'I'm sure he was,' said Tam.

'What about his sheep?'

'They'll be alright.'

For some reason the conversation then came round to Mr McCrindle.

'I wonder what Donald's done about his account not being settled,' I said.

'He'll probably allow him three months' grace,' said Richie. 'That's what usually happens.'

'How do you know that?' I asked.

'I live on a farm don't I? They never pay their bills on time.'

We considered what might happen in Mr Perkins's case, and all agreed that his account would most likely be sent to his home address, and was therefore nothing to do with us.

All this put us a bit behind with Mr Hall's fence, so as soon as Richie had collected his hammer from up the slope, we went back down to the lower fields to get as much work done as possible before dark.

Later on, when we were back in the caravan, Tam said to me, 'Are you seeing your woman tonight, then?'

'No, don't think so,' I replied.

'Too much for you, was she?'

'Yeah. Too many hormones.'

'We'll go to the Queen's Head then?'

'Alright.' I didn't particularly want to run into Marina again, nice girl as she was. Neither was I in the mood for long debates about where we were going to spend Saturday night. So the Queen's Head suited me OK.

'How much money have we got left?' Tam went on.

'We?' I said.

He was beginning to regard me as some kind of bank. I took some notes from my back pocket.

'That's all there is until Mr Hall pays up,' I said.

'Bet you've got some more stashed away,' said Richie.

'That's got nothing to do with it,' I replied. 'This is all the cash I've got.'

'Third each,' said Tam.

'Well, that's it. After that, nothing, so don't come running to me.' I counted out a third each for Tam and Richie, and pocketed the remainder. 'Don't forget we've nearly run out of food too,' I added.

'Yah, we'll get something,' was all Tam had to say. I noticed there was no mention of skittles and beer.

All the same, we spent a moderate night in the pub. It seemed the message was finally getting through to Tam and Richie that the cupboard was bare. There was no free beer from any quarter this evening, and while the locals swilled at a rate appropriate for a Saturday night, Tam, Richie and me were forced to make each beer last an hour. Given the right conditions, this can be a very pleasant pastime. There is a certain art in allowing a newly poured pint of beer the correct amount of time to settle, and then savour every drop by drinking at a gentle pace. But this is only an enjoyable process when you can afford to buy another pint as soon as the previous one runs out. When it's forced upon you by economic necessity it can become a grim affair. Tam and Richie certainly didn't look as if they were enjoying their Saturday night much. It seemed a poor reward for all the work we'd done. Still, with a bit of luck, Mr Hall would come up with the money as soon as we finished his job. I suppose the alternative would have been just to drink at the normal rate until the cash ran out, and then go home. This would have meant going to bed about half past nine, which seemed a bit early. Instead, we eked out the evening as best we could, and hoped we would be able to summon the energy to finish off Mr Hall the next day.

It was a dull moment when I woke up the following morning and heard the returned sound of rain on the caravan roof. I lay there listening as the water trickled off the gutter. I knew Tam and Richie were awake because they were both moving around in their beds. The caravan was moving from the outside as well, which meant that the wind had got up in the night and was swaying us about. The occasional splash of rain against the window confirmed this. I turned over in my bed and stared at the carpet, still damp from the last rainy period we had had to endure. It was clear none of us wanted to get out of bed. Nevertheless, we had to do a lot of work today. I realized that there was only one way to get Tam and Richie sufficiently motivated.

'Ah well,' I said. 'Should get paid today.'

Murmurs came from under the covers.

'We'll be able to have a good night tonight,' I added, trying to sound enthusiastic.

'On a Sunday?' grunted Richie.

I got up and made a pot of tea. When it had brewed I poured out three mugs and placed them on the worktop between the sink and the stove.

'Tea up,' I said.

'Pass mine over then,' said Tam, from his bed. I ignored him and took my tea over to my corner. Tam then attempted to reach over to the worktop without getting out of bed, with the result that he spilt most of his tea on the carpet. This was enough to make Richie get up and quickly claim the remaining mug. Tam, meanwhile, drank his dregs, retreated under his bedclothes and attempted to go back to sleep. I now decided it was time to freeze him out of bed by opening the door wide and leaving it like that. As the climate inside the caravan began to assimilate with the outside world (which did not take long), Richie and I made ourselves breakfast from the dwindling stocks. Eventually, as an apparent gale tried to funnel its way into our tin dwelling, Tam said, 'For fuck sake!' and got dressed.

Now that we were all up it seemed safe to make another pot of tea which we could enjoy properly before setting off for work. When at last Richie and I reluctantly started to pull on our waterproofs, Tam tried to remember what he'd done with his fertilizer sack.

'There it is,' said Richie, pointing out through the door. The sack now lay in a puddle across the yard, flattened by rainwater and looking completely unwearable. Tam resigned himself to getting soaked today, but retrieved the sack all the same. He looked in the wardrobe. Inside were a number of wire coat-hangers that jangled every time anyone moved around the caravan. He hung his sack up on one of them and closed the door. Moments later water began running out of the wardrobe.

'You should have shaken it out first,' I said.

'Too late now,' he replied.

Yes, I agreed, it was too late now.

This more or less set the tone for a miserable day's fencing. In our various states of attire (me in full waterproofs, Richie in his semi, and Tam wearing the remains of his leather jacket) we eventually got started. We'd taken on Mr Hall's job in a moment of heady optimism, but now we were confronted with reality, in the form of a field of mud. Rubber boots may be effective for keeping water out, but they have little resistance against suction, and we were constantly being pulled up by boots which refused to move, or which came off altogether. This made building the fence quite exhausting. Worse, Tam's lethargy seemed to be deepening all the time. It had clearly occurred to him that most of the money he would earn from Mr Hall would go straight to me and Richie, and by the time we got to the final section of the fence he'd lost interest altogether. He still just about managed to swing the post hammer with the required force, but in between posts he stood immobile and bedraggled, leaning on the shaft, while Richie got the next one ready. In this way we struggled on for the whole day, and only stopped when it was too dark to do anything else. We then went back to the caravan and attempted to dry out in front of the tired gas fire. We now had no money left, and the food supply was down to basics. I hadn't bothered to ring Donald and ask for our wages because we were supposed to be getting cash from Mr Hall. I now realized that we had no idea where he lived, and therefore were completely dependent on him turning up. We couldn't even go to his shop, because it was bound to be closed on a Sunday. And so, as condensation formed on the windows, we sat in the caravan and festered.

We'd all dozed off to sleep when headlights appeared outside. A door slammed and there was a knock on the door.

'Come in,' I said, as we blinked awake. The door opened and in came Mr Hall, again wearing the butcher's coat. As he stepped into the caravan the whole structure creaked under his weight.

'Can you build pens?' he said.

'Well, yes. Pens? What sort of pens?' I replied.

Tam and Richie were both struggling to sit up on their beds.

'We need some pens at the factory,' said Mr Hall.

'What factory?' I asked.

'Our factory,' he replied. 'Meat packing, pies and sausages. We've got the school dinners.'

I was still half asleep, and most of the oxygen in the caravan seemed to have been devoured by the gas fire. I couldn't take any of this in.

'You've got the school dinners?' I repeated.

He raised his voice. 'Yes! Now I'm going to ask again. Can you build pens?'

There was the usual silence from Tam and Richie, so I decided for them.

'Yes, I suppose so.'

'That's good,' he said, his voice quieter now. He paused for a moment, glancing round the caravan before speaking again. 'Get that fencing done alright, did you, lads?'

As he said this he smiled. It was obviously something he wasn't used to doing because stress lines appeared around his mouth.

'Just a couple of hours' work in the morning,' I replied.

The smile vanished. 'What do you mean?'

'Well, there's just a bit to do,' I said.

'It was supposed to be done by Monday.' Mr Hall was raising his voice again.

'Yes, well, we'll finish it in the morning.'

'I said by Monday, not on Monday! I want to put the beasts in there tomorrow!' In the course of this last sentence his face went red and his eyes began to blaze. I had never seen anyone lose their temper so quickly.

'I promise you, first thing . . .' I started, but it was no good.

'YOU SAID YOU COULD DO IT BY MONDAY! THAT'S WHAT YOU SAID! WELL, I'M NOT HAVING IT!' he roared, and slammed out of the caravan.

I tried to chase after him, but couldn't get my boots on in time.

'Mr Hall!' I shouted from the doorway, but it was too late, he was already driving away.

'Suffering fuck,' said Tam, obviously lost for words.

'You didn't ask him for our money,' said Richie.

'Nor did you,' I replied. 'Now what are we going to do?'

'Don't know.'

It certainly looked like we'd blown it with Mr Hall, so I went down the phone box to ring up Donald about sending some money urgently. There was no one there, so I had to leave a message. When I got back to the caravan Tam and Richie looked at me expectantly, as if a phone call to Donald would solve everything. When I shook my head, conversation turned to new speculation about Mr Hall.

'He must have been working today,' suggested Tam. 'That's why he had his white coat on.'

'Yes,' I said. 'But at the factory, not the shop.'

'He was in a bad temper before he got here,' said Richie.

We all agreed about that.

'He should have a day off,' remarked Tam.

'What's all this about pens?' Richie went on.

Obviously Mr Hall had another project in mind for us when he turned up, but during his ensuing rage he forgot all about it. Building pens would make a change from fencing and we quite liked the idea, but now it seemed the opportunity was gone. We wondered why they couldn't build their own pens.

'It's outside work, isn't it,' said Tam, by way of explanation.

'So?' I asked.

'English people don't like working outside, do they?'

'Well, I've been out in it all day,' I said. 'And I'm English.'

Tam looked at me. 'I know that,' he said. 'But you've been with us, haven't you?'

Next day, after a wretched night, Tam refused to have any more to do with Mr Hall's fence. I pointed out we had no choice but to finish the job, or we definitely wouldn't be paid, yet Tam was adamant.

'There's no point,' he said. 'We'll never see him again.'

Finally, he agreed to work alone on the hill while Richie and I went round to do the finishing off for Mr Hall. Tam was still lying in bed when this agreement was concluded, but he assured us that he would be getting up very soon and would make his own way up to the hill. I didn't want to waste any more time on this, so we left him to it.

Completing a fence always seemed to take longer than expected, and it wasn't until gone eleven that we were satisfied with it all. Apart from mud sticking everywhere we were quite pleased with the final result. There was no sign of Mr Hall's beasts arriving, so maybe he had changed his plans. When we got back to the yard we expected to find Tam still asleep on his bunk, but he was nowhere to be seen. Richie nodded in the direction of the hill. 'He'll be working up there,' he said.

I hoped he was right.

Tam was supposed to be getting straining posts dug in for the next section of the encircling fence, and when we got there we indeed found one newly erected post. No sign of Tam though. I left Richie doing the next post and took a walk along the fence line. The ground undulated as I walked, and just after a slight rise on the flank of the hill, I came across a disturbing sight. Tam was on all fours, a wood chisel in his hand, apparently sneaking up on a grazing sheep. Most of the other sheep were dotted around further up the slope, keeping, like sheep generally do, as far away from people as possible. This one, though, was engrossed with a particular area of grass, and for the moment had forgotten about personal safety. I was still far enough away for neither Tam nor the sheep to be aware of my presence. I stood still and watched. Tam slowly advanced on the sheep, chisel raised like a dagger, getting within a few yards of the animal. Then suddenly he sprang forward.

'Tam, no!' I yelled.

The sheep instantly bolted, and Tam fell forward onto the ground. He was still sitting there as I approached.

'What are you doing?' I said.

'I was just seeing if I could catch it, that's all,' he replied.

'Why?'

'In case we have to eat them.'

'Why should we have to do that?'

'Well, there's fuck all else, is there?' He looked desperate.

'Don't worry about that,' I said. 'We'll get some money soon from somewhere or other.'

I made Tam promise not to kill, or practise killing, any sheep, and we got back to work.

That day I concentrated hard on keeping Tam and Richie going. I was worried about the job grinding to a halt again, especially as we'd done all that work for Mr Hall and not a penny to show for it. Morale was understandably very low, and I had to cajole and encourage the two of them all day. Finally, as the light faded, we set off back to the caravan. We'd got some work behind us at last, and felt better for it. The only problem, as Tam had pointed out, was that we hardly had any food left. As we approached the yard I happened to mention that there were two remaining cans of beans in the cupboard under the sink. This was enough to trigger a race back to the caravan between Tam and Richie. They leapt out of the truck and charged across the yard. Both of them got to the caravan door at the same time, and a noisy struggle followed as each tried to force his way inside. With a violent crash they both fell through the doorway, and a moment later became unusually silent. Wondering what had caused this sudden transformation I stepped inside the caravan. Donald was sitting on the end of Tam's bed.

10

'Glad to see you're making full use of daylight hours,' he said.

'Oh, er, yes,' I replied. 'Where's your truck?'

Donald had a truck similar to ours which he used as a general runaround for visiting gangs on site. There was no sign of it in the yard, which was why we'd been taken by surprise.

'Robert dropped me off,' he said. 'He's borrowing it for a couple of days.'

'A couple of days?' I repeated.

'Yes,' he replied. 'In the meantime I'm going to stay here with you as this job doesn't seem to be going very quickly.'

Tam and Richie had sat down on the spare bunk opposite mine. I glanced at them. They both appeared to have gone pale.

'You people really should be getting on faster than this,' Donald went on. 'After all, there's no great hardship here.'

'We've run out of money,' I said.

'What happened to the float I gave you?'

'Spent it.'

'Well, if you've "spent it" you would normally be expected to go without.'

'Oh.'

'But it's fortunate for you that I've brought your wages with me.'

This, at least, was a relief. It was supper time and we decided to cook everything we had left, the beans and one or two other things, all together in a big pan. Donald just about hid his disgust as a suitable pan was selected from the sink and scraped clean. I thought it would be a good lesson for him to see how I had to live every day. However, once the pan was cooking he seemed to take a more positive interest in what we were having for our tea.

'That smells nice,' he remarked.

'Yes,' I replied. 'But there's only three plates.'

It then transpired that Donald had brought his own plate, a special disposable one that did not require washing up. Reluctantly I gave him a dollop and we all sat and ate.

'Very nice,' said Donald afterwards, reaching for his overnight bag. 'Now then. Wages.'

He produced three pay packets. 'Oh, by the way,' he said. 'This came to the office.' He handed me an invoice. It was the bill for the repair to the post hammer.

'Oh, yes, right,' I said. 'I wondered what happened to this.'

'I thought you'd better see it,' said Donald.

'Thanks,' I replied. 'This would normally be settled out of the float, I suppose?'

'I'm afraid not,' replied Donald. 'The float only covers general wear and tear. Negligent damage has to be deducted directly from your wages.'

And he made the deduction, in cash, on the spot.

After he'd given out the pay packets Donald said, 'I expect you'll all be dashing off to the pub now?'

'Not really bothered,' replied Richie. He was reclining on his bunk, reading *An Early Bath for Thompson* again, from page one.

'I'm surprised,' said Donald. 'I thought you'd be out every night.'

'Actually, I'm saving up for Christmas,' said Tam.

'Well, I'm sure the company can afford to stand a round of drinks,' announced Donald, and a few minutes later he was driving us to the pub, all squashed together in our truck.

On the way out he paused next to the original Hall Brothers fence.

'I see someone else is working round here,' he said.

'Yes,' I replied. 'Local company, I think.'

'Well, we don't want to go stepping on their toes, do we?' Donald got out of the truck and carried out a brief examination of the Hall Brothers' fence. We watched as he stood at one end and genuflected, glancing along the line of posts.

'Hmmm. Exemplary,' he said, as he rejoined us.

It was quiet at the Queen's Head when we trooped in. Donald led the way to the bar and ordered four pints while Tam, Richie and myself held back a little. While he was pouring the drinks Ron the landlord raised his eyebrows at me. I nodded in reply. Whether this exchange had any significance I don't know, but Ron kept his distance during the evening, and didn't poke round asking his usual questions.

We sat down at our normal table in the corner, with an extra chair for Donald. It was an odd evening. Donald seemed to think that we would want to talk about fences all night, so he kept on starting up conversations on the subject. We learnt about all the new fencing techniques that were being developed by the company and its rivals, and we heard how many yards of fencing had been erected by other gangs in different parts of the British Isles.

'How many gangs are working in England?' I asked.

'None,' replied Donald. 'You're the only one, although Robert has gone to look into getting more work down here.'

Judging by the expressions on their faces, Tam and Richie didn't like the sound of this.

'By the way,' Donald continued. 'There's still been no word from Mr McCrindle.'

'Oh,' I said. 'Hasn't there?'

'He's gone very quiet. Not even a phone call, which is quite surprising. He's rather fond of his telephone and rang me up on a daily basis while his fence was being built.'

Donald had now turned his gaze upon Tam, who shuffled awkwardly on his seat.

'Did he?' he managed to say.

'Indeed he did,' replied Donald. 'I asked him to keep his beady eye on you and he was most obliging.'

'Helpful of him,' I remarked.

'Yes, I thought so too, and he turned out to be very equal to the task. Which is why I'm going to allow him three months' grace to settle his account.'

'That's . . . er . . . good.'

All the while, we were concentrating on drinking our beers at the correct speed. Donald's offer on behalf of the company to buy a round of drinks had been ambiguous and caused uncertainty among us. We weren't sure who was expected to pay for the second round, or any subsequent ones for that matter. As a result we drank 'in line' with Donald, making sure none of us emptied our glasses before he did. Donald drank at a very slow rate, which was proving to be a form of torture for Tam and Richie, and, to a lesser extent, me. The last two inches took for ever, but eventually Donald drank up, closely followed by the three of us.

'Same again?' he said, taking us all by surprise. He went up to the bar again. This was the first time me, Tam and Richie had been alone since his arrival.

'Just act naturally,' I said.

When he came back with the drinks Donald resumed the discussion about fences, but in spite of this Tam and Richie began to look a little happier as the beer went down. Richie remembered that he'd run out of fags, so he went off to get some and came back with two packets. He and Tam then sat and quickly smoked several in a row. Donald looked at Richie as he lit up yet again.

'Why do you abuse your body all the time?' he asked.

'Because no one else will do it for me,' replied Richie.

Next thing Tam was up at the bar buying another round, and I realized I was going to have to talk to him fairly soon about his mounting debt problem.

Back at the caravan a space had to be found for Donald to sleep, and it was decided he would occupy the bunk underneath Richie. There was a jumble of used clothing lying there which Richie grabbed in a great armful and stuffed behind his pillow. Donald opened the wardrobe and was confronted by Tam's fertilizer bag, now dry and stiff on its hanger. He slid it back along the rack, and hung up his shirt in front. As we prepared for bed Donald said, 'No late evening coffee, then?'

'I'm afraid not,' I replied.

In the dead of night I woke up for some reason, and lay

listening to the others as they slept. Over the last few weeks I had got used to the noises Tam and Richie made in their sleep, and I recognized them instantly.

Richie, who always lay on his back, produced a sound similar to the underwater gurgling of an old motorboat. Meanwhile, at the other end of the caravan, Tam seethed like a distant ocean.

Donald, however, in the bunk closest to mine, was totally, totally silent.

I planned to impress Donald in the morning by being the first to get up, but when I awoke I saw he was already moving about the caravan, apparently making tea. He stood looking at the piled-up sink, and then produced a clean mug from his bag.

'My mug's up there,' I said, pointing to the cupboard above my bunk.

'Really?' Donald replied, and poured himself a tea.

Donald's presence certainly made a big difference to the speed we arose that day. There was no question of Tam lounging about in bed until the last minute, and we were ready for work by half past seven. Donald had his own map of the job, with all the fences marked out in red ink, and the first thing he did was go for a tour of inspection, accompanied by me. We followed the hill up to the summit, and then came down by way of the cross-fence, Donald all the time checking for wire tension and, of course, straightness. When we got to the encircling fence he seemed quite satisfied with what he'd seen.

'Hmmm, quite professional,' he said.

After a while we came to the gateway that stood alone. Donald looked at it for a moment, and then said, 'Yes, I always think it's better to do the gate first and build the fences round it.'

Donald had put on some overalls, and it soon became clear that he intended to work alongside us during his visit. He organized us into two small sub-gangs, one pair erecting posts, the other fixing wires, and then swapping round every couple of hours. This grouping worked quite efficiently, and a long stretch of fence was built on Donald's first day. It was interesting watching him work with the post hammer. His action resembled that of a machine. How his bones must have jarred every time he brought the hammer down accurately, but stiffly, on top of each post. He did not allow himself any 'give', but instead transferred all his energy directly into the hammer. In this mechanical way Donald completed yet another line of posts, while his chosen assistant struggled to keep up with him.

That night in the pub I found myself at the bar buying a round of drinks. It was at this point that I noticed Ron the landlord behaving oddly. Instead of placing the newly filled glasses on the counter between me and him, he put them about two feet to my left. At the same time he stared hard over my shoulder in the direction of the corner table where Donald, Tam and Richie were sitting. I was about to pick up the four pints in a clutch, so I would only have to make one journey from the bar, when Ron produced a tray. Onto this he began loading the glasses, still eyeing the corner, and moving sideways, until, at last, I realized he was attempting to line me up with Donald. He seemed to be trying to obscure himself from view, so I decided to stay where I was and let him adjust his position to mine. Suddenly he glanced down at the counter, and at the same time I felt an envelope being pressed into my hand. I nodded and slipped it into my pocket. He visibly relaxed as I took the tray and carried it over to the table, where Donald and the others were discussing fencing. The envelope remained in my pocket for another half hour, after which time I casually strolled out to the gents. Locking myself in the cubicle, I examined the mystery package under a dim light. There was no writing on the envelope and it was unsealed. Inside was some cash, large denomination notes of exactly the sum agreed for Mr Hall's fencing. I looked for some kind of written message but there was nothing, just money. When I returned to the bar room, conversation had dried up. This was the normal state of affairs for Tam and Richie, who were generally content to sit with their pints and say nothing. Being accompanied to the pub by Donald had imposed considerable stress on them, and they looked quite relieved when I rejoined the table. It had been even worse for them during the day, when Donald organized us into two pairs and they had been forcibly separated. Each of us had worked with one of the others, so that the different tasks were shared fairly. When Richie was selected to go off with Donald to erect a new line of posts he looked as if he was embarking on a death march. Tam's turn came later, and he seemed like a broken man when he came back.

'How long's Donald staying for?' he asked me.

'Until Robert comes to collect him . . . a couple of days,' I replied.

'But he's been here two days already.'

'He only arrived last night,' I said. 'It just seems longer, that's all.'

Now, hours later in the pub, there was still no let-up. The three of us were trying to unwind over a few beers, but Donald had something to say to us.

'You people really should start thinking in terms of efficiency,' he began. 'Building a fence is quite simple. First you dig in your straining posts at each end, and tighten a wire between them. This gives you a straight line along which you set the pointed posts (point downwards). Then you fix and tighten the remaining wires, one by one, and the job is complete.'

While Donald was speaking I looked at Richie, sitting opposite me. His eyes had slowly closed and his head nodded forward, and he now sat motionless next to Tam, who stirred uneasily.

'What about adding the support strut at each end?' I asked.

'That goes without saying,' replied Donald. He reached into his jacket and took out some papers.

'I've prepared some hand-outs for you,' he announced, passing them round. 'They contain all the main points you should bear in mind during the construction process.'

Richie resurfaced and focused on his copy. I looked at mine. It consisted of step-by-step diagrams of how to build a fence, with little stick men doing the work. Donald now turned to me.

'You should also operate a stricter regime inside the caravan,' he said.

'I take it you're referring to the squalor,' I replied.

'Correct.'

'Well I don't see how I can force people to be hygienic,' I

said. I noticed that Tam and Richie were now studying their hand-outs with great interest.

'Domestic arrangements fall within your remit,' said Donald, after which the subject was dropped.

The evening came to a natural close when the pub shut, and as we got up to leave, Donald noticed that Tam had left his hand-out on the table.

'Don't forget this,' he said, picking it up.

'Thanks,' said Tam, stuffing it in his back pocket.

Next morning, as we prepared for another day of efficient fencing, Donald said, 'Robert should be turning up this afternoon.'

Tam and Richie didn't respond to this news, but when they went out to load up the truck with the day's gear I could hear them whistling. Even better, Donald allowed them to work together for the entire morning, pulling out and tightening wires, while I paired up with him to knock some more posts in. We made good progress, and by mid-afternoon another line was complete. Donald had taken the post hammer, and I had been his assistant, spacing out and setting up the posts. As we stood looking at the finished work, we saw that one post clearly wasn't level with the rest, and needed knocking in a little further.

'I'll do it,' I said, taking hold of the post hammer.

I liked to use the 'full swing' method, same as Tam, so I planted my feet firmly on the ground and held the hammer at arm's length. Then I swung it over in an arc and down onto the post. It was a good solid blow, but another one was required, so I repeated the action. This time the hammer seemed unusually light as I brought it over, and at the end of the stroke

I realized that the head had flown off and I'd been left holding just the shaft. At that moment something sniffed my boot. I looked down and saw Ralph saying 'hello' in the way dogs do when they've just arrived. There was a movement behind me, and I turned round to discover Donald engaged in a strange embrace with Robert. It looked as if one was teaching the other to dance.

'Oh hello, Robert,' I said, but instead of his usual polite greeting I got no reply. In fact, Robert was very quiet indeed.

Then I noticed the missing hammer head lying on the ground.

'Direct hit,' said Donald. I could see he was struggling to hold Robert upright, so I stepped forward and together we leaned him against a post. Donald examined him closely.

'How is he?' I asked.

'That's irrelevant,' Donald replied. 'He's dead.'

He took the shaft from me and inserted it in the hammer head. It was loose.

'That's one bill we won't be paying,' he said.

'What are we going to do with Robert?' I asked.

'We'll have to bury him,' replied Donald.

'Shouldn't he be buried in Scotland?'

'Normally, yes,' he acknowledged. 'But in this case it's too far.'

He took the fence plan from his pocket and studied it. 'He'll have to go under the next gateway.'

'We'll get Richie to do it,' I suggested. 'He's best at digging.'

'Alright,' said Donald. 'Tell him it's best to put Robert under the slamming post rather than the hanging post.'

'Is there a particular reason for that?' I enquired. It seemed a good moment to settle the point.

'Not as far as I know,' he said.

When Tam and Richie had finished what they were doing they came wandering along the fence line to join us, and Donald pointed out that they should have taken the opportunity to move their gear round to the next section.

'Never a wasted journey,' he said.

After we'd told them about Robert, Tam voiced concern over who would look after Ralph.

'I'll take him with me,' announced Donald.

By the time Robert's gateway was finished the light was quickly failing, so we made our way back to the yard. The company truck was parked next to the caravan where Robert had left it. In the back was a spare post hammer which Donald let us borrow while he got ours 'repaired properly in Scotland', as he put it.

Donald had some tea and then prepared to leave before it got too late. When departure time came I said, 'Well, thanks for all your help the last couple of days.'

'That's alright,' he replied. 'Of course, I'll have to quarter it from your final costings.'

I was not sure what he meant by this, but I could guess.

Donald looked around the farmyard. 'I was hoping to have a few words with Mr Perkins while I was down here,' he said. 'But he seems to be keeping a low profile.'

'I've hardly seen him myself,' I said. 'It was dark when we first got here.'

'So I heard,' replied Donald. 'Now, I'll expect this job to be wound up fairly quickly. You won't want to be coming back after Christmas to finish it, will you?'

I hoped not. Time had sneaked up on us and it was now December. No wonder the days were so short and the nights so long. Donald's visit had pulled us along a bit, but there was still a fair amount of work to be done before we could escape from Upper Bowland. I told Donald I would do my best and we said our goodbyes. By this time Tam and Richie had joined us in the yard. Donald opened the door of the company truck and Ralph jumped in beside his new master. Then they were gone.

'I'm fucked if I'm coming back after Christmas,' said Tam, as we slumped into the caravan.

'We should be alright if we press on at the same rate,' I replied.

Tam looked at me. 'You don't believe in all this efficiency shite, do you?'

'Well,' I said. 'It worked OK while Donald was here, didn't it?'

'That's because he's a fucking robot,' said Richie.

Yes, I thought to myself, he quite possibly is.

To stop Tam and Richie going into decline I quickly produced Mr Hall's money and we shared it out. Tam again settled his debts, and again found himself with virtually nothing left. However, we all had enough to go to the pub, which is what we did.

'Get that cash alright, did you?' asked Ron as he served us our beers. Seeing that it was him who handed it to me this seemed a pointless question, but I politely replied, 'Yes, thanks.'

'I hear you're going to be building some pens,' he added.

'You've seen Mr Hall then, have you?' I said.

'He's been very busy,' replied Ron. 'They've got the school dinners.'

We sat at the corner table and considered this vague information. Obviously the Hall Brothers had further plans for us, but until they made contact we would have no idea what exactly was involved. In the meantime, we had to get on with our own job. I wasn't sure what effect the approach of Christmas would have on Tam and Richie. On the one hand it might spur them on so we got finished in good time, but on the other it could just make them homesick and unable to concentrate on work. I must admit that even I felt slightly marooned as the tail lights of Donald's truck headed off towards the road. When we returned to the caravan late that night, the hill above us seemed to be brooding in the darkness.

There were no further sightings of the Hall Brothers over the next few days, so we plodded on with our own fence. At first Tam and Richie marched around 'being efficient' and doing things as Donald would have liked, but I knew the sham wouldn't last. They preferred to take a laissez-faire approach to the work, tackling jobs as they presented themselves, rather than in a set order. The fence would still get built, eventually, but at about half-speed. I decided to go along with all this. After all, I had to live with Tam and Richie twenty-four hours a day, Donald didn't.

On the day we finally got the job finished we received a visit from John Hall. Once again we'd all dozed off to sleep after a hard day's work, when the headlights swung into the yard. I was ready for him, however, when he stepped into the caravan, which made the usual protest under his weight.

'Are you ready to do these pens, then?' he began.

'Yes, I think we can spare a couple of days,' I replied.

'That's good,' he said. 'I've bought the timber already.'

'Oh. Have you?'

'Yes. I got two hundred railway sleepers in a job lot.'

When he said this I detected a shock wave running between Tam, Richie and myself.

'Railway sleepers?' I tried not to sound surprised.

'Best things for building pens with,' said Mr Hall. He was probably right, but I wondered what we were letting ourselves in for. Two hundred railway sleepers! That was more than a couple of days' work.

'What will we be doing then, exactly?' I enquired.

'Building pens,' he replied with irritation. 'I just told you.'

'Yes, but where?'

'At the factory. So we can bring beasts in direct from the field.'

'Er . . . that's illegal, isn't it?' I said.

Mr Hall eyed me. 'Are you trying to tell me how to conduct my affairs now?'

'No, but . . .'

'What?' He looked as if he was about to explode again.

'Nothing,' I said, surrendering.

'Good. Now let's have a bit of common sense round here.' His features had relaxed again. 'It'll be cash in hand as before, and there'll be grubbage for you at the canteen.' Mr Hall was certainly magnanimous in victory. He glanced at Tam and Richie. 'Alright, lads?'

Obliged to speak at last, they both mumbled, 'Thanks.'

I fell in with this change of mood. 'I gather you've got the school dinners,' I said, hoping he would enlarge on the subject.

'Yes, we have,' he replied. 'Right. I'll expect you tomorrow morning.'

He opened the door to leave.

'By the way,' I asked. 'Where is the factory?'

'Lower Bowland. You can't miss it.'

The factory turned out to be a large shed of corrugated steel at the end of a long track. The building had a look about it that suggested it had been erected without planning permission. All around were fields, in which unsuspecting cattle grazed behind newish HALL BROS. fences. On the side of the shed was a block-house canteen and some offices. When we arrived we found David Hall parked in his lorry, waiting for us. There were also a few butchers' vans nearby. As I said before, David Hall was much easier to deal with than his brother. He actually appeared friendly and had little difficulty smiling.

'I've got the sleepers on the back here,' he said. 'We'll have a bit of breakfast and then you can get them unloaded.'

We'd all had breakfast before we left the caravan that morning, but none of us said anything as he led us into the canteen, where a number of butchers, all in white coats, were already seated. There was a choice of sausages fried, grilled or baked, served up by a man in a cook's apron who seemed to bear the Hall Brothers' family resemblance. He appeared to be running the kitchen single-handed. When not dishing out sausages he spent much of his time attending to the griddle behind the counter, while occasionally replenishing the tea urn. After we'd had a plateful of sausages each we sat and drank mugs of tea while David Hall talked to us about fencing.

'Hard job, fencing, isn't it?' he began.

'It's OK,' replied Tam.

'Must be repetitive knocking all those posts in, though. First one, then another, then another after that.'

'You get used to it,' I said.

'Yes, but repeating the same thing over and over again. Enough to drive you mad. All that repetition.'

The more he went on like this, the more it began to sound as if he didn't know what he was talking about.

'I thought you did all the fencing work round here?' I said.

'It depends what you call work,' he replied. 'There's work-work, and there's telling other people to work. I prefer the second one.'

'So you're not a fencer yourself then?' I asked.

'Hoo hoo! Course not!' he said, grinning.

The lorry was still waiting to be unloaded when we went outside again.

'John's got a plan of the pens somewhere,' said David Hall. 'I'll just go round the office and get it. You can start unloading if you like.'

'Thanks,' I said.

The railway sleepers were stacked lengthways, so Tam and Richie climbed up on the lorry to pass them down, while I remained on the ground. There was a certain way of unloading timber which made the work quite straightforward. It involved the law of gravity. In this case it was simply a matter of Tam pushing each sleeper along the stack until it tipped over, to be upended by Richie, who in turn slid it off the back of the lorry. It would then land upright, ready for me to lower onto the new stack. For a while this procedure worked quite well, and we began to develop a steady rhythm. However, as my stack on the ground got higher, I needed a little more time to move each sleeper into position. Tam and Richie didn't seem to realize this, and actually started to send them down faster and faster. In the end I had a relentless stream of heavy railway sleepers coming at me, and it was starting to get a bit much.

'Can you slow down a bit!' I shouted. 'One of these is going to hit me in a minute!'

I didn't like having to raise my voice to Tam and Richie, but sometimes it was more than justified. Their response was to stop work and have a fag. This gave me time to catch up on the ground, and when I'd got sorted out I had a rest too.

'This is going to be a fucking slog,' remarked Tam.

Yes, we all agreed, it was. If we were going to build a proper substantial structure then all the uprights would have to be dug into the ground to give them strength. We hadn't seen the plans yet, but we knew that there'd probably be dozens of holes to dig. Then there was the question of holding it all together. You couldn't just nail railway sleepers to one another because they were too big. They'd have to be drilled and fastened with coach-bolts to keep them secure. I wondered if Mr Hall had allowed for this and got a supply. Somehow I doubted it. We quickly came to the conclusion that the job would take more than a couple of days, and when David Hall came back with the plans our worst fears were confirmed. These were going to be heavy-duty handling pens for all manner of beasts. It would take us a week at least, maybe more!

Of course, we didn't express our doubts in front of David Hall, and indeed spent the rest of the day laying out the railway sleepers according to their positions on the plan. But as soon as we left the premises that evening Tam said, 'I think we should just fuck off.'

'What, you mean abandon the job?' I asked.

'Fucking right,' he replied. 'Otherwise we'll never get home.'

Richie, of course, agreed with Tam, and I have to admit that it didn't take long for me to come round to their way of thinking. We'd definitely over-stretched ourselves by agreeing to build those pens, and the best course of action was to just clear off. So when we got back to the caravan we immediately began to make preparations to leave. We decided it would be best to go straight away and travel overnight, with me and Richie sharing the driving. So while they packed up the caravan and hitched it to the truck, I went on a final tour of inspection of Mr Perkins's fence. It seemed a long time since we had first set eyes on that huge pile of posts and wire in the farmyard. Now it had been transformed into a taut, gleaming structure that glinted in the moonlight. I made sure all the gates were left closed, so that nothing could escape, and then rejoined Tam and Richie. Not long afterwards we hit the road.

It was quiet next morning when we pulled into the company premises and parked outside the tool store. We sat in the cab for a few minutes while Tam and Richie had a smoke.

'Right,' I said when they'd finished. 'We'd better have a go at sorting out all the gear.' We got out and stood looking into the back of the truck. The collection of tools lay in a shallow pool of rainwater, some of them bent, most of them showing the first signs of rust. This was supposed to be a set of professional fence-building equipment, but actually looked like a hoard of junk. There were hole-digging implements, wire-tightening gear, a rusty steel spike (blunt), a selection of chisels and a chain winch. All in various states of disrepair. Also several coils of wire. The only item that appeared to be in reasonable condition was the post hammer, lying slightly to one side.

'Here's Donald,' murmured Tam, and they both immediately began sorting through the gear. Donald had emerged from his office and was advancing across the yard in our direction. His sudden appearance had a marked effect on Tam and Richie, whose faces showed that they were concentrating hard on their work. Tam leaned over the side of the truck and pulled out the post hammer.

'Glad to see it's still in one piece,' said Donald as he joined us. He took the hammer from Tam and stood it, head downwards, on the concrete. Richie, meanwhile, had lifted one of the coils of wire onto his shoulder and was about to take it into the store room.

'You seem to be in a great hurry all of a sudden,' said Donald.

This caused Richie to hesitate awkwardly in mid-step with the coil balanced on his shoulder. He half-turned and looked at Tam. Donald was now peering into the back of the truck.

'You people really should take more care of your equipment,' he said.

After a dutiful pause Richie made another move towards the store room, but was again brought to a halt by Donald.

'Leave that for now. I've just had a serious phone call. You'd better come into the office.' Without further comment he turned and walked off towards the open door. We all glanced at each other, saying nothing, and filed after him.

A very powerful naked light bulb hung from the office ceiling. Beneath it, Donald had placed two hard chairs side by side facing his desk. They were slightly less than full adult size, made from wood, and had been positioned squarely and symmetrically in the middle of the floor.

Tam and Richie did not have to be told where to sit.

12

How long Donald kept them sitting there, side by side on those two hard chairs, was difficult to say. There were no clocks in that office, no calendar on the wall. Even the limited daylight coming through the small recessed window was defeated by the glare of the light-bulb, further isolating the office interior from the world outside. Donald sat silently behind his desk, holding Tam and Richie under his gaze. Meanwhile, the radiator pipe beneath the floor did its work. The only sound was the occasional shuffling of feet as they unstuck their warmed-up rubber boots from the lino. Then, at last, Donald spoke.

'I've just had your mother on the phone,' he said. 'She was in a call box and sounded rather distressed.'

Richie had adopted his usual position and sat with his arms folded, gazing at the desktop. Now he was forced to look directly at Donald.

'My mother?'

'Yes.'

'Did she say what it was about?'

'Yes she did. It seems she hasn't heard from you the entire time you've been away.'

'Oh,' said Richie. 'No.'

'No letters, postcards. Nothing.'

'I told her I'd be back around Christmas.'

'Rather vague, was it not?'

''Spose.'

'And in the meantime you sent no word.'

'No.'

'Well, I know how she must feel,' said Donald. 'I find myself in the same situation. I get no tidings from No. 3 Gang for days on end. Not one phone call. No sign of a progress report. Nothing. Then suddenly you turn up here, unannounced, out of the blue. It's like the Retreat from Moscow.'

Richie said nothing.

'Why didn't you telephone before you came back?' said Donald.

The room remained silent. All this time I'd been casually leaning on the radiator by the window, watching the interrogation but feeling somewhat detached from it. The two hard chairs had been set up for Tam and Richie, therefore I was exempt. Or so I thought. It was only as the silence persisted that I realized Donald had now turned his attention to me.

'Why didn't you telephone before you came back?' he repeated.

'Forgot,' I replied. Even as I spoke I knew this was a pathetic excuse.

'You forgot.'

'Yes.'

'Your first duty as foreman is to liaise with me, yet you forgot.'

'Yes. Sorry.'

'It would be a different story if I forgot to pay you, wouldn't it?'

I noticed that Tam and Richie were both looking over their shoulders at me, and suddenly I felt like a schoolboy being rebuked by his teacher in front of the whole class. I'd seen them being put through the mill in this way several times, but always considered myself somehow immune. Now it dawned on me that I was no more 'in' with Donald than they were. The post of foreman brought no benefits, only problems. In fact, it was beginning to seem like some sort of purgatory.

There was a long silence and then Donald said, 'I think it's time you became acquainted with the Demonstration Fence.'

He rose from his chair and gave a low whistle, at which Ralph emerged from beneath the desk. Tam patted his head once or twice, and then Donald led us all outside. We followed him across the yard to a gate, which he held open as we passed through. Away in the middle of the field I could see a structure glinting in the pale winter light, and as we approached I saw that it was a short fence about thirty yards long, standing alone. This fence served no apparent purpose, because it was possible to walk round either end.

'How long's this been here?' I asked.

'Just a few weeks,' replied Donald. 'This is our Demonstration Fence.'

'Who built it?'

'Me. I did.'

I should have known really. This fence was more or less perfect. All the posts stood erect and unblemished in a dead straight line. The joinery had been done perfectly too, so that each straining post and strut appeared to be an integral unit. Even the wires seemed to be highly polished.

As soon as we got there Donald went to one end and glanced along the line of posts, genuflecting as he did so. As a mark of respect I did the same thing, followed by Tam and Richie.

I noticed a small yellow sign fixed to one of the straining posts. It bore the company name and telephone number. Also the words CAUTION: ELECTRIC FENCE.

Donald turned to Richie and said, 'Give me your hand.'

'What?' said Richie.

'Give me your hand.'

Richie glanced at Tam, who had moved away from the fence slightly and now stood looking very hard at the yellow sign, as if trying to memorize the telephone number. Richie slowly held his hand out. Donald took it in his own left hand, and seized the top fence wire with his right, causing the two of them to jerk in time for several seconds. Finally, Donald let go of the wire and released Richie.

A stunned silence followed, after which Donald said, 'Why didn't your rubber boots save you?'

Richie looked at him for a long moment before replying. 'Don't know.'

Donald turned to Tam. 'Do you know why?'

'Because you're not wearing them,' said Tam.

We all looked down at Donald's feet. He was wearing ordinary leather boots.

'Correct,' said Donald. 'The electricity went to earth through me.'

'Didn't you get a shock as well?' I asked.

'Oh yes,' replied Donald. 'I got a shock.'

We stood looking at the Demonstration Fence in solemn silence.

'This is the way forward,' announced Donald at last. 'The permanent electric high-tensile fence. The final solution to the problem of the restraint of beasts. The electricity teaches them to keep away from the structure, so that there is virtually no wear and tear. And if the electricity should fail, the high-tensile wires act as a barrier. Now, do you want another demonstration?'

'No, that's alright, thanks,' said Tam.

'You'll be learning all about the electric high-tensile fence in the next few days,' said Donald.

'Will we?'

'Yes. We've had several enquiries about it already. You'll be going to England in the New Year to build one, so it's important that you know what you're doing.'

Tam was about to say something, but Donald looked at him and he remained silent instead.

'Any problems with that?' said Donald.

'No, no,' replied Tam.

Donald whistled Ralph, who sat some distance away, having declined to approach the fence, and we walked back across the fields towards the company premises. When we got into the yard Donald said, 'By the way, have you got a measurement for me?'

'Oh, yes,' I replied, and retrieved Mr Perkins's file from the truck. On the outside of the file I'd written the final length of the fence at Upper Bowland.

'I take it you had no further problems down there,' said Donald.

'None to speak of,' I replied.

As I drove Tam and Richie home we had a discussion about the electric fence.

'I don't like the sound of it,' remarked Richie.

'Nor me,' said Tam. 'We should do high-tensile and nothing else.'

'I suppose Donald's going to make us go in over Christmas to learn about it,' I said.

'I'm not fucking going in over Christmas,' Tam snapped.

'Aren't you?'

'Fucking right I'm not.'

'It's just me and you then, Richie,' I said.

'Are you going in then, Rich?' said Tam.

'Suppose we'll have to won't we?' replied Richie. 'If Donald says so.'

I slowed the truck down and turned up the gravel track leading to the golf course. Rounding a bend we came upon Tam's father operating a saw bench.

'Stop here,' said Tam, and we pulled up and watched.

Strewn on the ground around Mr Finlayson were a number of newly-cut larch poles, all about ten feet in length. He was using the circular saw to sharpen the end of each pole into a point. The safety cover on the bench had been discarded, and the huge blade spun unprotected as he worked. It was a noisy operation. The saw was attached to a diesel power plant, and the combined din of the engine and the blade cutting into the timber had drowned out the sound of our truck. Mr Finlayson took each pole, swept it across the blade several times to create a point, and then threw it up on a stack beside him. He was concentrating on his work and remained unaware of our presence.

Tam carefully opened his door and got out of the cab. Then he slowly began moving in a circle until he was directly behind his father. He waited until another pole was complete, and then, at the exact moment Mr Finlayson threw it onto the stack, he leapt forward with a wild cry and seized his arms, locking them with his own, and holding his head forward. Then Tam slowly bent his father down, forcing him to kneel in the sawdust until his head was an inch or so from the spinning blade. After holding him in this position for several seconds Tam let go and stepped back quickly. Mr Finlayson moved cautiously away from the blade before standing upright and looking round. Richie and I had both got out of the truck to watch this 'sport', and when he caught sight of us he shook his head and closed down the machinery. Then quick as a flash he seized a pole from the stack and hurled it at Tam, who had to jump out of the way to avoid being hit.

'That could have been a very nasty accident,' said Mr Finlayson. 'Now pick it up and put it back on the stack.'

Tam obeyed.

Mr Finlayson looked at me. 'How are you?' he said, removing handfuls of wood shavings from his pockets.

'Alright, thanks,' I replied.

'Still foreman?'

'Er . . . yeah. Just about.'

'Well, that's good for you, isn't it?'

' 'Spose.'

'They don't usually last this long.'

Mr Finlayson used his son's return as a signal to finish work. He replaced the safety cover on the saw bench and began counting the completed poles.

'What are these going to be for?' asked Tam.

'I'm building a stockade round the house,' replied his father.

'Why?'

'To stop you coming home any more.'

Richie was very quiet as we left the golf course behind and carried on towards his place. I realized this was the first occasion he'd been separated from Tam for quite a while, and wondered how he would cope. Who would he share his fags with, for example? It was hard to imagine Tam without immediately thinking of Richie, and vice versa. I remembered back to that time I'd asked Tam where Richie was and he'd said, 'We're not married you know.' Well maybe they weren't, but they spent more time together than most married people. No doubt they'd be together again very soon (when the Crown Hotel opened), but in the meantime Richie had to face his mother. I expected her to be angry with him for not writing home or anything, but when we pulled into the farmyard she appeared in the doorway with a very worried look on her face. Mrs Campbell was clearly most concerned about something.

'Oh Richard,' she said. 'I think there's been a terrible mistake.'

'It's alright,' he replied. 'I'm home now. What happened?'

'Oh dear. I don't know how to tell you.'

'Has someone died?'

'No, no. It's about the electric guitar.'

'What about it?'

Mrs Campbell hesitated and then said, 'A man from the catalogue came and took it away.'

13

Richie went quite pale. 'You mean it's gone?'

'I'm afraid so.'

'When?'

'This morning.'

'Didn't you pay the instalments?'

'I kept them all up to date, but we didn't think you were coming back.'

'Why?'

'That's what your employer told us.'

'What, Donald?'

'He didn't give his name, but he said he hadn't heard from you for quite some time. Therefore he didn't think you were coming back.'

'Therefore?' said Richie.

At this point his mother began weeping.

'Oh Richard!' she wailed. 'We didn't mind you having the guitar! Really! We'd have got used to it soon enough. Your father could go out and see to the cows, and I've got my Reading Circle. Please don't think we did it on purpose!'

As Richie tried to comfort his mother, and she him, I noticed Mr Campbell quietly regarding the scene from an outhouse doorway. When he saw me looking he withdrew again.

'As soon as I turned my back for five minutes,' said Richie. 'Gone.'

That night, as the three of us sat in the Crown Hotel, Tam listened solemnly while Richie told him his bad news.

'The man from the catalogue took everything, did he?' he asked at length.

'Everything. The guitar, the amp. Even the instruction manual.'

'For fuck sake.'

'I'd only had it a few weeks,' said Richie. 'I'll probably never see it again.'

'At least you won't have to pay off any more instalments,' I pointed out as a sort of consolation.

Tam considered the case and then passed judgement. 'This wouldn't have happened if we hadn't had to go to England,' he announced.

'Yeah, but Donald's behind it all,' I added.

'He's getting worse and worse,' said Richie.

We all agreed about that.

'And to think they only started off building fruit cages,' said Tam.

'Who?' I asked.

'The company.'

'Did they?'

'That was before your time. Or yours, Rich. Raspberries mainly.'

'To stop them escaping?' asked Richie.

'Er . . . no. Not really . . . no.'

Tam went to the bar to get three more pints, and on returning said, 'Christmas Eve tomorrow.'

'Yeah,' I said.

'I suppose we've got to go into work, have we?'

'Suppose so,' I replied. 'Donald hasn't said anything.'

'Fuck sake.'

'Maybe he'll let us finish early,' I suggested.

'Huh,' said Tam.

Christmas Eve didn't start particularly well. It would probably have been alright if Donald hadn't intercepted us almost as soon as we arrived for work. This gave us no chance to prepare ourselves for what he had in mind. We were sitting in the truck while Tam and Richie had a pre-work smoke, carefully watching Donald's office door as the minutes passed. When they'd finished we were going to go and report for duty, but Donald got to us first. He suddenly approached from the direction of the tool store, and next moment he was peering at us through the cab window as we sat there side by side.

'Have you been out to the Demonstration Fence since we last spoke?' he asked.

'Not yet,' I replied.

'I'm surprised,' said Donald. 'It's in your own best interests to become familiar with the technique as quickly as possible. Our schedules have been brought forward and you'll be on your own very soon.'

'Will we?'

'Very soon indeed. It's imperative you understand how to build a permanent electric high-tensile fence. I hope you're all wearing your rubber boots again today?'

We confirmed that we were.

'Good,' said Donald. 'It looks like rain so you'd better don your waterproofs. I'll be back in a moment and then we can have another lesson.'

We got out of the cab and started scrabbling about putting on our wet weather gear while Donald disappeared into his office. The condition of Tam's leather jacket had got beyond a joke. Apparently he'd put it in his father's boiler room to dry out overnight, and now the fabric was desiccated and even less resistant to rain than before. Still, the jacket was all Tam had so he stuck with it. Donald, of course, was perfectly equipped. When he emerged from his office he was wearing a complete set of waterproofs, complete with hood, and a pair of thick-soled rubber boots. He signalled for us to follow him and we again set off across the fields. I noticed there was no sign of Ralph this morning. It had started raining by the time we got to the Demonstration Fence, and standing there in the wet, it appeared even brighter and newer than it had on the previous occasion.

'So,' said Donald. 'Where does the electricity come from?'

Good question. The Demonstration Fence resembled an

ordinary high-tensile fence in every way. Only the yellow warning signs showed that it was different. It stood alone and apparently unconnected to anything else. We watched as beads of rainwater gathered along the wires before dropping into the grass.

'Suppose it must come from underground,' I suggested.

'Correct,' said Donald. He led us to one end of the fence and indicated a black cable emerging from beneath the turf.

'Insulation is provided by a hardened rubber sheath,' he explained, reaching for the cable, taking hold, and disconnecting it from the fence.

'By the way,' he went on. 'This is the sort of tension you should be achieving on all occasions.' Donald seized a fence wire and pulled it towards him. There was hardly any give at all.

I was about to test the tension for myself, but changed my mind.

'You're quite safe,' said Donald. 'The power's not connected. Even if it were, your rubber boots would protect you from all but the slightest shock.'

'I don't trust it yet,' I replied.

'Come, come,' said Donald. 'You're in more danger of being struck by lightning on a day like this.'

I looked at the black cable, to check that it had definitely been disconnected from the fence. Then I breathed in and gripped the wire.

'Hmm. Quite tight,' I said, letting go again.

'Yes, I'm quite pleased with it,' said Donald, and he began carrying out yet another thorough examination of the fence. I was beginning to come to the conclusion that he was obsessed with the thing. He tested the tension of each wire, and ran his hand over the timber to ensure the joinery was perfect. Finally, he stood at one end and genuflected, glancing along the line of posts to see that it was straight. When Donald was satisfied he reconnected the electricity.

'Now there's a quick and simple way of finding out whether the power is switched on,' he said.

Donald bent down to the ground and broke off a blade of grass. Holding it between his thumb and forefinger, he touched the top fence wire. At once a faint ticking sound could be heard. Donald moved the blade up a little, and the ticking grew louder. Then he turned to Tam.

'Do you want to try?' he said.

All the time we'd been at the Demonstration Fence, Tam and Richie had remained somewhat aloof, keeping well clear of the structure and not taking part in any of the tests.

'It's OK,' said Tam. 'We usually let our foreman do that kind of thing.'

'And what if your foreman ever leaves the company?' asked Donald. 'What will you do then?'

'Don't know.'

'You're not afraid of this fence, are you?'

'No, no,' replied Tam, breaking off a blade of grass and gingerly touching it to the fence.

'Good,' said Donald. He glanced at me. 'The question was purely hypothetical, of course. I don't ever expect you to leave.'

This was very reassuring.

'Now there's a small task I'd like you to carry out over the next few days,' Donald continued. 'I want you to dig a trench from here to the company premises, so we can put the cable deeper underground.'

'Isn't it deep enough already?' I said.

'Oh no,' said Donald. 'Nowhere near deep enough. It's barely beneath the surface at present, placed there as a temporary measure. Quite unsatisfactory. I want it buried deeper.'

'How deep?'

'So that it can be forgotten about.'

'Oh.'

'You know how to bury things, don't you?'

'Yeah, 'spose.'

'Good. Besides, it'll give you all something useful to do over Christmas.'

I was aware of a wave of disappointment flowing between Tam, Richie and myself.

'All you'll need is a spade each,' said Donald, 'and while we're in the tool store I have something else to show you.'

He led us back to the company yard and opened the door to the store room. At once the ticking noise could be heard again. We went inside, and as our eyes became accustomed to the gloom, we could make out a metal box mounted on the wall, on which a small orange light was flashing.

Apart from the ticking noise, the tool store was a quiet place, a sort of inner sanctum of the fencing trade. Rows and rows of tools lined the walls, most of them familiar to us. There were large post hammers, all with wooden shafts and identical cast iron heads. There were deep-digging tools, some in the form of simple long-handled spades, others doubled into tongs. Nearby stood steel spikes which could be used for piercing starter holes in the ground, or for levering out awkward stones. Hanging from hooks on the wall were sets of wire-pulling devices, complete with chain winch and gripper. There were boxes in the corner containing brand new gear still wrapped in stiff grease-proof paper and not yet assembled for use. Other tools had been tried and rejected, such as the deep diggers which opened the 'wrong way' and which no one could get used to. Finally there was the unrecognizable specialist equipment, acquired for some particular reason or other, but whose purpose was not apparent.

And now there was something new in the tool store. A metal box ticking on the wall with an orange flashing light.

'This is the transformer,' said Donald. 'One of these can deliver electricity for an entire network of fences.'

'Really?' I said.

'Several miles actually. Mr Hall was most impressed.'

The transformer continued ticking, but all else was silent.

'Who?'

'Mr Hall. That's the new client. He's shown a great deal of interest in the Demonstration Fence.'

'So he's been here, has he?' I managed to say. Tam and Richie remained very, very quiet.

'He attended a demonstration, yes,' replied Donald. 'It seems that the permanent electric high-tensile fence matches his requirements perfectly. Mr Hall is just the type of person I had in mind when I devised the system.'

'Is that where we're going after Christmas?' I asked.

'Correct.' Donald cast his eye along the rows of equipment lining the wall and then said, 'By the way, I take it your personal tool sets are all intact?'

There was a pause and then Tam said, 'I need a new hammer.'

'That comes as no surprise,' said Donald. He stepped towards a bench by the wall, on top of which was a drawer full of hammers. 'Would you like to select one?'

Tam picked one at random and said, 'This'll do me.'

Donald took the hammer and balanced it carefully in his hand.

'I'm surprised,' he remarked. 'I'd have thought someone of your experience would have been a little more discerning.'

Tam lifted a second hammer from the box.

'Alright. This one,' he said.

'That's better,' said Donald. 'Of course, you understand the cost will be deducted from your wages?'

'Thought so,' said Tam.

Now Donald turned to Richie, who was leaning against a stack of cardboard boxes.

'May I?' he said.

Richie quickly moved out of the way, and Donald lifted a box down. Inside were a dozen or so leather belts, each with small loops attached. He chose two and gave them to Tam and Richie. (As foreman, I already possessed such a belt.)

'These should help to prevent any further loss of equipment,' said Donald.

The belts were well made, each loop designed to carry a certain item, such as a hammer, wood chisel or pair of wire cutters.

'They'll also make you look more professional,' he continued. 'This is only the first stage of our future plans. In the forthcoming year there will be a simple uniform for you to wear. The designs are not yet complete, but I have in mind some sort of overall bearing the company insignia.'

Tam had already fastened his belt and fitted the new hammer into an appropriate loop. Meanwhile, Richie stood awkwardly holding his in one hand.

'Are these going to be deducted from our wages as well?' he said at last.

'No,' replied Donald. 'Consider them to be a Christmas gift from the company.'

'Thanks,' they both mumbled. Donald fitted the lid back onto the box and replaced it on the stack. Then he turned to me.

'So.'

'Do you want us to start the trench today?' I asked.

'The sooner you start the sooner you'll finish,' he replied. 'Don't forget your spades.' And with that he left us. We stood in stunned silence in the tool store as he crossed the yard back to his office. Then, without a word we each took a spade and trooped out into the rain, through the gate and across the field.

It was only when we were well away from the company premises that Tam spoke at last. 'For fucking fuck's fucking sake,' he said. Richie and I knew exactly what he meant.

And so on that soaking wet winter day we began digging our trench. We dug it deep and we dug it straight. We worked with rain running down our necks and our hair bedraggled. Mud clung to our boots, the turf became slippy, and rainwater ran freely along the bottom of the trench. Daylight began to fail early, but still we pressed on, knowing that Donald could make an appearance at any moment. It was only when the coming of darkness made it impossible to do any more work that we packed in.

'What a fucking way to spend Christmas Eve,' said Tam. 'We could have been in the pub all afternoon.'

'This is worse than last year,' said Richie.

'What happened last year? I can't remember.'

'We had to go to Robert's house for a glass of sherry.'

'Oh that's right. I forgot about that. Got a fag, Rich?'

Richie found his cigarettes in a dry place beneath his waterproof, and squeezed into his soaking jeans for the lighter. I realized for the first time that I no longer found the ritual irritating.

When we got back to the yard the light was on in Donald's office. We discussed calling in to say 'good-night' and even 'Have a nice Christmas', but none of us was really in the mood.

'Fuck it,' said Tam. 'Let's go home.'

What sort of Christmas was it going to be? Not only was there that trench to complete when we came back, which was two or three more days' work at least, but we also had the prospect of facing Mr Hall again. Nobody had mentioned Mr Hall all afternoon because it just didn't bear thinking about. We'd worry about that when the time came, and no sooner. In the meantime, the lights of the Crown Hotel offered some consolation. Even Donald couldn't expect us to work Christmas Day and Boxing Day, and I seemed to spend much of the festive season in the Crown with Tam and Richie. So did a large part of the local population, including Morag Paterson.

On Boxing Day night Richie, Billy and I were sitting at one of the large tables waiting for Tam to come back from the bar with a round of drinks. He'd got engaged in a conversation with Morag and was taking his time, but who could blame him? I'm sure I'd have done the same thing if I had her full attention. The Crown Hotel was certainly a better place with her there.

In the end Billy lost patience and shouted, 'Hurry up, Tam!'

Unfortunately this triggered off an incident involving their father. Mr Finlayson had been sitting alone at the end of the bar for most of the evening. Apparently unaware of his sons' presence, he was gazing at the mirror behind the whisky bottles, his right hand holding a pint of heavy, his left hand gripping the counter. When he heard Billy's voice he looked round and caught sight of Tam standing further along the bar, still talking to Morag Paterson. Next moment he was on his feet and lurching towards them.

'Here we go again,' murmured Billy.

Mr Finlayson had plainly been drinking a lot, and swayed to and fro as he stood facing Tam.

'We could have done all the fencing round here!' he roared.

'Who?' said Tam.

'Us! Me! And your brothers!'

'What's he talking about?' said Morag, giggling. Half the pub was now listening to the exchange.

'Nothing,' said Tam. 'Pay no attention to him.'

'Finlay and Son!' announced his father in a loud voice.

Jock appeared behind the counter and tapped it twice with his finger.

'Alright, Tommy,' he said. 'That's enough of that.'

But Mr Finlayson was now in full swing. 'We could have had it in the bag! Proper genuine stock fencing! Solid! None of this low-cost, high-tensile shite killing the market! Us! Me! And your brothers. And instead of that . . .' He was beginning to falter. 'And instead of that you went over to the other side!'

At that moment some helping hands launched Tam's father through the doorway and out into the night.

'What it needs is a stockade!' he bellowed in the darkness. 'Right around the house!'

As the hotel door was closed and bolted, Tam brought our drinks over to the table. 'Sorry about the delay,' he said.

'What was your dad getting worked up about?' asked Richie.

'Nothing of importance,' replied Tam. 'He thinks he's an expert on fencing all of a sudden.'

'That's as bad as my father,' said Richie. 'He hasn't touched his fences for years and now he's started going on about getting them all renewed.'

'Well can't you do them?' asked Billy.

'That's what I said,' replied Richie. 'But he goes "Oh no, they've got to be specially matched to my requirements."'

'What's that supposed to mean?' said Tam.

'Fuck knows.'

'Sounds like the sort of thing Donald would come out with,' I remarked.

Jock was going round the tables collecting empty glasses, and when he got to us he said, 'I hear you're going back to England.'

'How did you know that?' said Tam.

'Ah well, word gets around you know,' replied Jock. 'You'll be better off down there this time of year.'

'Why?'

'They don't have proper winters, do they?'

'Suppose not, but we're not going yet. We've got Hogmanay first.'

Ah yes, New Year's Eve, that was the next big thing to look

forward to. As Jock continued his rounds we squeezed what we could from the remaining dregs of Christmas. A few minutes later the bell rang for last orders and Richie went to get them in.

'I'll just see if Morag wants a drink,' said Tam.

But she'd already gone.

Returning to work the following day we found out how Donald had spent his Christmas. There was no sign of activity anywhere in the company yard, so we collected our spades meaning to carry on with the trench where we'd left off. The rainy weather had subsided into clear stillness and there was a slight frost lying across the fields. As we approached we could see the Demonstration Fence glinting in the winter sunlight, but there was something different about its appearance. Drawing nearer we saw that during our absence the original fence had been extended. There was a new section at each end, at right-angles, so that the structure now formed three sides of a square. Again the work was done perfectly, with flawless joinery and unblemished posts in dead straight alignment.

'Why's he done it like that then?' said Tam.

'Don't know,' I replied.

'How does he get the wires as tight as this?' Tam gripped the wire. There was a ticking noise and he leapt back from the fence. 'For fuck's sake, it's switched on!'

'You should have done the test,' I said.

'Fuck the test!' he snapped. 'That's it. I'm not going near it any more.'

'Here's Donald,' said Richie, and we all began studying different aspects of the Demonstration Fence with interest. Donald had just come through the gateway at the corner of the field and was advancing towards us.

'I bet he turned it on deliberately when he saw us coming to have a look,' said Tam.

Yes, I thought, he probably did. Donald was walking along the line of our trench as he approached, peering into it from time to time, no doubt checking that it was sufficiently deep.

'Glad to see you managed to return so promptly after the festivities,' he said as he joined us. 'I was beginning to think I had a band of truants on my hands.'

'Oh,' I said. 'No.'

'Well, you seem to be making reasonable progress with your excavation work. Three or four more days should see it completed.'

I nodded towards the Demonstration Fence. 'You've been busy then.'

'Yes,' replied Donald, and began once more to make a thorough examination of the shining structure. We trailed vaguely after him as he patrolled the three adjoining sections.

'Is it going to be a square when it's finished?' I asked.

'Correct.'

'With a gate?'

'No gate.'

'But if someone was inside, and it was switched on, they couldn't get out.'

'Quite,' replied Donald. 'Remember, it's for demonstration

purposes only.' He allowed us a few moments to absorb the remark, and then said, 'Any other questions?'

'Where's Ralph?' asked Tam.

'We've lost him.'

'Have we?'

'I'm afraid so.'

'How?'

'There was an accident during the early trials.' Donald laid a hand on one of the straining posts. 'He's under here if you wish to pay your respects.'

14

It took us the rest of the week to get that trench completed. Every day we turned in for work, collected our spades from the tool store and carried on digging. In other circumstances we could have probably wound the job up in two or three days, as Donald had estimated. After all, there were no particular problems to overcome. Now that the weather had dried up the work became less like drudgery, and we were able to apply ourselves to it properly. As a result the trench was neat, with straight vertical sides and a flat bottom. It actually made a nice change from building fences all the time. I soon came to realize, however, that Tam and Richie were pacing themselves so that we didn't get finished too quickly. This was all to do with the approach of New Year's Eve. I think they suspected that if we got the trench done any sooner Donald would send us off on the next job and they'd miss all the fun. As it turned out they needn't have worried on that account. After a couple of days Donald paid us our wages (minus certain deductions) and announced that he was off to prepare the site for Mr Hall's new fence. As usual he gave no indication about when he would be coming back, but nevertheless a relaxed atmosphere soon developed. Not long after he'd gone we went to the tool store and switched off the transformer. There would be no more surprise electric shocks for the next few days at least. Then we carried on with the trench, but at about half the speed we'd been going before, with regular fag breaks and pauses for general speculation. In the end we had the work finished by New Year's Eve. Oddly enough, Donald did not return for quite some time. This was most unusual. He rarely left the office unattended for very long, yet on this occasion it was almost a week before we saw him again. Whatever was delaying him at the Hall Brothers' place must have been very important.

'Maybe he's fallen into their sausage machine,' remarked Tam. We all had a good laugh about that.

In the meantime New Year's Eve came and went. It was the usual story in the Crown Hotel. Leslie Fairbanks provided music for a packed house, while Jock clattered and complained behind the counter. Tam and Richie got pissed with Billy, and everyone ignored Mr Finlayson, drinking alone up at the bar. For some reason, Morag Paterson failed to make an appearance, which I for one found disappointing. The evening was pleasant enough all the same. I was 'allowed' to sit at Tam and Richie's table, although I knew I wouldn't be able to keep up with their rate of drinking for very long. My solution to this problem was to drop out of a few rounds, and not claim a drink, but then Tam accused me of 'back-watering' which I thought was a bit unfair. He punished me by buying me drinks I didn't want, so that I spent New Year's Day with the worst hangover I'd ever had.

The day after that there was nothing officially to do at work, but I persuaded Tam and Richie that we should go in and get the caravan cleaned up, to which they reluctantly agreed. It was in an even worse state than I remembered. All the carpets were still damp and the drainpipe from the sink had somehow become disconnected. Also the tyres had gone down again. I got Tam to pump them up while Richie dragged out the carpets and hung them on a line to dry. Meanwhile I tested the electric strip light to see if it still buzzed. It did, loudly, but I decided to take a power cable with us next time anyway, because the gas lamps were on their last legs and I didn't want to live in the dark.

We were just having our break when a truck suddenly pulled into the company yard. Donald was back. He got out and stood regarding the caravan in its dismembered state.

'Looks like you need a bit of a sort out,' he said, by way of greeting.

'We're waiting for the carpets to dry,' I explained.

'I see.'

Tam and Richie were now busy fiddling about with the waste disposal pipe under the sink. As Donald peered at them through the caravan window I said, 'You were gone a long time.'

'Yes,' he replied. 'I got delayed.'

'Oh, er . . . anything serious?'

'A minor project of Mr Hall's needed urgent completion and he asked me to oblige.'

'What sort of project?'

'I've been building pens.'

'What, on your own?'

'Not quite. I took an assistant with me.'

There was a low gurgling noise as the waste pipe came away in Tam's hand. Richie quickly tried to jam a bucket underneath, but it was too late and filthy water gushed across the kitchen floor. Donald turned away.

'I take it you got your trench work completed OK?' he continued.

I assured him we had.

'Good,' he said. 'Everything's ready at Mr Hall's and we want to get you shipped off tomorrow morning.'

It struck me that Donald sometimes employed a very unfortunate turn of phrase. He was forever talking about 'rounding us up' and 'shipping us off' as though we were being transported to some sort of penal colony or corrective camp, rather than merely going to undertake a commercial contract. Tam, Richie and myself were quite used to his ways of course, but it must have sounded very odd to potential customers.

'What are we doing for this Mr Hall then, exactly?' I asked.

'Something rather special,' replied Donald. 'He wishes to eliminate all possibility of escape. Therefore we're providing him with electric fences of extended height.'

'How high?'

'Seven feet.'

'That's a bit over the top isn't it?'

'Not really,' said Donald. 'Oh, by the way, you'll need to be at Mr Hall's place by six o'clock tomorrow evening.'

'Why's that then?'

'After that you'll find the gates are locked.'

It was still dark when Richie and I arrived at the golf course the following morning to pick up Tam. I stopped the truck some distance from the greenkeeper's house, bibbed the horn and wound up my window. Then we waited for signs of movement in the kitchen, where a single light-bulb shone. As we sat there waiting it seemed to me that the place looked different from before, though I couldn't quite see why. The house no longer had a proper outline, and appeared instead to be part of a vast backdrop. Even the light cast from the kitchen window came to an abrupt end after a few yards, as if blocked out by some kind of solid barrier. I flicked the headlights onto main beam, and we saw a newly-built stockade advancing round the back and sides of the house. The work was not yet complete, but nearby a huge stack of larch poles lay ready, each with a pointed end.

'Blimey,' I said. 'I thought he was joking.'

'You don't know Mr Finlayson,' said Richie.

Just then there was a movement in the darkness. An upper window of the house had been opened and a haversack was dropped to the ground. Soon afterwards a figure in a leather jacket emerged. We watched in silence as Tam lowered himself down until he was suspended from the ledge by his hands. After hanging there for several seconds he seemed to change his mind and started to pull himself up again, but then lost his grip and plummeted into the gloom.

We heard a thud and a 'Fuck' in the near distance, waited a moment longer, then Tam appeared in front of the truck, grinning.

'Misjudged that a bit,' he said.

'Why did you come out the window?' I asked.

''Cos my dad's in the kitchen.'

'So?'

'That's reason enough. Come on, let's go.'

'Richie!' roared a voice from the direction of the house.

'For fuck sake,' said Tam. 'It's him.'

'Richie!' shouted the voice again. 'Come and have a cup of tea!'

'Ignore him,' said Tam.

'Richie!'

'I'll have to answer him,' said Richie. 'He knows I'm here.'

Tam tutted.

'Oh, hello Mr Finlayson!' Richie called.

'Come and have a cup of tea while you wait!'

'I've just had one at home, thanks!'

'It's already poured!'

'I'll have to go and be polite,' said Richie, getting out of the truck and trudging towards the house. 'Bring that foreman with you!' yelled the voice.'

Tam looked at me. 'You'd better go in,' he said.

I followed Richie through the blackness to the kitchen, where Mr Finlayson was waiting.

'Can't have you sitting out there, can we?' he said. 'Your tea's on the table, I've put sugar in.'

'Thanks,' I said.

'He'll be down in a minute.'

'Oh . . . er . . . right.'

We sat awkwardly at the table and tried our teas. Richie took sugar normally but I didn't, and it was very sweet. I didn't say anything though. A few moments later there was a rattling sound in the upper part of the house, and shortly afterwards Tam came down the stairs into the kitchen. His jacket was badly scuffed up the front, and most of the fabric had pulled away from the lining.

'Is that you then?' said his father. 'These two have been waiting.'

'I know, I know. Hi.'

'Hi,' we both said.

We rose from our seats and moved to go, but Mr Finlayson was blocking the door. 'Finish your tea first,' he ordered. Then, to Tam, 'You'll have to do without.'

There was a dutiful pause as we quickly drank our tea, then Mr Finlayson moved aside from the doorway and allowed us to leave.

It was beginning to get light when we arrived at the company premises to collect the caravan. The first thing we saw was a large articulated lorry being loaded up in the timber yard. There were huge posts stacked along its entire length, and still more were being added. An air of efficiency prevailed. The whole place was emblazoned with artificial light from two floodlamps mounted high up on the gable end. I'd never noticed these before, and they made the company premises resemble an industrial plant, rather than a collection of converted farm buildings. The lorry had its own powered crane, which was being operated by someone on the far side. Only the steel toe-capped boots of this individual could be seen moving around, and he in turn was being given instructions by someone entirely lost from view. This made the entire process seem to have nothing to do with us.

'Look at all those posts,' muttered Tam. 'We'll be away for months.'

'Looks like it,' I said.

Soon after we'd begun hitching up the caravan, Donald appeared from the direction of the timber yard and asked me to go into his office. Lying on the desk I noticed a cardboard carton stamped with the words 'Caution: electrical appliance'. Donald produced a file and handed it to me.

'You'll be dealing with a Mr John Hall,' he announced. 'The full client name is Hall Brothers, but this Mr Hall is head of the regime and you should take your instructions from him. The other brothers are little more than sleeping partners.'

I changed the subject and indicated the carton. 'Is that for us?'

'Correct,' said Donald. 'As foreman it will be your responsibility to install the transformer before carrying out the final tests. Have you made yourself entirely familiar with the system?'

'More or less.'

'Good. This fence consists of ten live high-tensile wires and four strands of barb, so the posts are quite long. You'll need to take a stepladder with you.'

I looked at Donald and tried to see if he was making a joke or not. Was he seriously expecting us to knock these posts in from the top of a stepladder? After a few moments I decided that, no, he wasn't joking.

'Sounds like a big job,' I remarked at length.

'Yes,' said Donald. 'Our largest contract to date.'

'Will any of the other gangs be involved?'

'There aren't any other gangs,' he replied. 'You're the last one.'

A shadow crossed the window as the lorry moved out of the yard. A few minutes later I found Tam and Richie sitting side by side in the truck, waiting to go.

'I suppose you haven't got any money,' I said.

'Nope,' said Tam.

'I've got a bit for the time being,' said Richie.

I went to the store room and found a stepladder. Then we set off.

That caravan was a flimsy affair. The walls were nothing more than a double layer of hardboard, separated by a timber frame and clad on the outside with tin plate. Only the chassis held it all together. And as I slowly came awake next morning the whole structure was creaking. Creak, creak, creak, it went. Rhythmically, creak, creak, creak. I lay with my face pressed against the wall, half-asleep, trying to remember where I was.

'Is that you doing that?' said Tam.

I looked beyond my toes and saw him eyeing me from his bunk.

'No, it must be Rich,' I murmured.

'Is it fuck,' said Richie. 'Someone's moving us.'

Outside I could hear an engine running. I pulled the curtain open slightly and saw a fence moving along outside the caravan. We were being inched slowly backwards, stopping and starting every now and then.

'That sounds like our truck,' said Tam.

'Fuck sake!' I said. 'I left the keys in!' I struggled out of my sleeping bag and stood up just as the caravan began a turn, so that I fell against the back window. Looking out I saw a convoy of vans, all the same, lined up in the road. There were men in white butchers' coats standing here and there amongst them, watching the activity around the caravan.

'They're inside,' somebody said.

The caravan stopped moving and moments later there came a curt knock at the door. I opened up and saw David Hall standing outside, wearing the same white coat as the others. He didn't look very pleased.

'There you are,' he said. 'We thought you'd gone off.'

'No, we were in here all night.'

'What did you block the drive for?'

'The gate was locked.'

'So?'

'We didn't know where to go.'

He grunted and peered past me into the caravan, where Tam still lay in his bunk.

'What's he doing?'

'Nothing.'

'Well he should be careful of lounging around when John gets here.'

At that moment a horn blasted at the back of the queue. Another vehicle had arrived, obviously impatient to get through.

'Here's John now,' said David Hall. 'I'm afraid he's going to take a very dim view of this, just when the vans are coming back from the night run.'

He gave a signal and the caravan was towed into a lay-by at the side of the road, with me, Tam and Richie still inside, trying to get our boots on. Then the vans were manoeuvred onto the grass verge so that the new vehicle could come by. John Hall's car moved cautiously along the line of vans, as if inspecting each one as it passed, and then stopped in the entrance to the driveway. It rocked slightly as he got out. The two brothers spoke briefly for a moment, and then came over to the caravan door.

'You were supposed to get here by six o'clock last night,' said John Hall. 'Didn't you know that?'

'Sorry,' I said. 'We tried, but we just couldn't make it.'

He looked at me for a long time before turning to his side. 'Take them to the pens, will you, David? That's the best place for them.'

15

There were two notices beside the entrance to the factory. The larger one bore the words HALL BROTHERS in red on a white background. The second notice, just below, was smaller and new. KEEP OUT it said.

As John Hall's car moved slowly off, followed by the procession of vans, David Hall turned to me and said, 'Not a very good start, is it?'

'Suppose not,' I replied. He seemed different somehow to the last time we'd met him. Much more serious. I considered trying to start up a bit of light-hearted conversation to redeem the situation, but I got the feeling it was a waste of time. He appeared to have given up on the banter and chit-chat he'd indulged in when we were here before.

'You're fortunate John didn't send you straight home,' he continued. 'Now then, you can give me a lift.'

Without saying anything else he went and sat in the double passenger seat of the truck. Tam and Richie had remained inside the caravan while all this was going on, so I shrugged at them and shut the door before joining David Hall in the cab. He sat in silence as I drove up the driveway to the factory, towing the caravan behind, and only spoke again when we arrived at the pens. 'You can park here.'

As I expected, Donald had made a perfect job of the pens, although how he'd done it in a week I didn't know. All those railway sleepers we'd unloaded now formed a substantial complex of enclosures and conjoining gates. It was a very professional job. Someone had recently been along and applied creosote to all the timber, giving it a spick-and-span look. There was a sort of holding area at the entrance, and this was where we were supposed to put the caravan. While Tam and Richie got it unhitched and jacked up, I asked David Hall if there was somewhere to plug in our cable.

'Of course,' he said, and disappeared into the factory.

As soon as he'd gone Tam came over to me and said, 'Not very friendly, is he?'

'Why should he be?' I replied.

After all, I thought, we couldn't really expect the Hall Brothers to be particularly friendly, could we? Not after we'd messed them about so much. Arriving late the night before hadn't helped, of course. We'd tried, but it was just impossible to get there any faster towing that caravan. Despite all his efficient calculations Donald never seemed to make allowances for this. Six o'clock had come long before we neared the end of our journey, and once we knew we weren't going to make it we'd given up rushing. Then Tam had started going on about 'cutting our losses' and stopping for a couple of pints at the Queen's Head. I'd said I didn't think it was a good idea going back there just yet. In the end Tam and Richie had agreed that we should pick up a few cans somewhere and forget finding a pub the first night. By the time we got to the factory it had gone nine, and the gate was locked. So we'd simply crawled into the caravan with our cans and spent the night there. Not a very good start.

I was just pondering all this when a small window opened at the side of the factory and an arm appeared. David Hall's podgy hand started waving about impatiently, so I quickly got the cable and fed it to him through the window. Then I gave the strip light a short test. As usual it buzzed loudly.

'Right. Meals,' he said, as he emerged again. 'Meal times are seven, twelve-thirty and six. You're just in time for breakfast if you're quick.'

This sudden announcement came as a pleasant surprise. Donald hadn't said anything to us about getting our meals at the Hall Brothers' place, and things immediately started looking better. We walked round to the canteen past the factory loading bay, where all the vans were now backed up with their refrigerator units rumbling. The bay was deserted: the men from the factory were having their breakfast. They took little notice of us when we entered the canteen. All they seemed interested in was guzzling platefuls of sausages and going back to the counter for more. The other Hall brother (who we later found out was called Bryan) was still there behind the counter, serving up sausages fried, grilled or baked. He dished out a good helping for each of us, and we found a spare table in the corner. I didn't realize how hungry I was until I started eating, and my plate was soon empty. The same went for Tam and Richie. We all went back for seconds, got a mug of tea apiece, and then sat there feeling fairly content with the world.

'Shame there's nothing but sausages,' said Tam as he finished the last one. 'A few eggs and tomatoes would have been nice.'

'Or mushrooms and a fried slice,' suggested Richie.

One or two people at nearby tables looked across at us as if we'd said something out of order. I watched over the rim of my mug as David Hall entered the canteen and came to our table. Tam and Richie had their backs to the door and were unaware of his approach. They both started slightly when he spoke.

'Finished?'

'Yes, thanks,' I said, placing my knife and fork neatly in the centre of my empty plate.

'Want some more?'

'Er . . . no. Thanks anyway.'

'Don't you like our sausages then?'

'They're very nice. But I've had two lots already.'

'I see.' David Hall was now standing very close to us. He turned and addressed Tam.

'What about you?'

'Same here.'

'You mean you don't like them either?'

'No, no . . . it's just that I've had enough. Thanks.'

By this time the general murmur in the canteen had ceased. Everyone had stopped eating, and sat listening to the exchange.

'Well, this is most disappointing,' said David Hall. 'We were under the impression you liked our sausages.'

'We do,' I replied.

'But you've just turned round and said you don't!'

'No.'

'Make your mind up.' He looked at the three of us for a few moments. 'Very well,' he said at last. 'If you've quite finished

I'd better take you over to the offices. John wants to see you before you begin work.'

The silence faded away as he led us out of the canteen. Bryan Hall was standing behind the griddle, and as we passed I nodded and said 'Thanks', but he just looked at me and said nothing.

David Hall showed us into a waiting room beside the offices and left us there while he went to find his brother. Looking out of the window we watched the men from the canteen drifting slowly back into the factory.

'Poor fuckers,' said Tam. 'Working here all the time.'

'Don't think I'd like it,' I said. 'What's that, Rich?'

'Not sure, really.'

Richie was gazing at a picture on the wall. There was nothing else to do, so I went over and had a look.

It was a framed drawing of a small boy adrift in a rowing boat. This was accompanied by a nursery rhyme:

> If Jack comes home at half past three
> Then he shall have some cake for tea,
> But if he's late and won't be quick
> We'll beat him soundly with a stick.

'Charming,' I remarked.

The door handle turned and John Hall came in, wearing a white butcher's coat.

'I gather you don't like our sausages,' he said.

'No,' I replied. 'Really. We do.'

'Doesn't sound like it. Not from what I've heard.' Mr Hall thrust his hands in his coat pockets and stared at the floor for some time. 'Still, I doubt if your opinion will count for much in the long run.' He glanced up quickly. 'You know we've lost the school dinners?'

'Oh,' I said. 'Sorry to hear that.'

'Yes, it's been very hard to bear.'

'Any chance of getting them back?' I asked.

'It's possible. That's why you're here, of course.'

'Is it?'

'Oh yes. There's plenty of room for improvement. Now you're not going to go running off again, are you?'

'Er . . . no.'

'"No", or "er . . . no"?'

'No.'

'I should hope not. Ah, there you are, David.'

David Hall had appeared in the doorway holding a clipboard.

'Everything's in order, John,' he said.

'Good.' John Hall signed a docket and then addressed us again. 'Now I think we might as well go for a stroll around the perimeter. These plans and diagrams are all very well, but you need to get a picture of the final enclosure for yourselves. Come on.'

He took us outside and round the end of the factory, where we passed the huge pile of new posts we'd seen on the lorry.

'The materials managed to arrived on time,' he said. 'But you didn't.'

The planned line of the new fence went along the extreme edge of the Hall Brothers' property, and was marked out by a series of wooden pegs in the ground, presumably put there by Donald. It was a relief to be back outside again and dealing with something I understood. After all that talk about sausages

and school dinners I felt as if I'd just undergone some sort of
cross-examination. Tam and Richie had got off relatively lightly,
but even they had a defeated air about them. I was quite looking
forward to getting back to work. First, though, we had to accom-
pany Mr Hall on his conducted tour. There was nothing much
to see. The land around the factory was already divided up into
several empty fields demarcated by existing fences. We paused
briefly by one of these, and I noticed it bore the silver HALL
BROS. tag.

'These were built by our own people,' said Mr Hall.

'Hmm, nice job,' I remarked, tugging a wire.

'Quite probably,' he replied. 'But they're insufficient for our
present requirements.'

'Does that mean we've got to demolish them?'

'No, we'll take care of that. You press on with the new fence.
The beasts will be here soon.'

I didn't bother asking what sort of 'beasts' required a seven-
foot-high electric fence. After John Hall left us alone Tam and
Richie had a fag and there was a lot of 'fuck saking' and so
forth. The job did seem a bit daunting, but I knew that once
we got started they'd most likely settle into it OK. So we collected the truck and went round the back of the factory for
some straining posts. These were enormous and could only be
lifted by two people. As we man-handled half a dozen onto the
truck it slowly sank down on its springs. Then we drove slowly
out to the fence line and began work. Tam and Richie got the
first post erected quite quickly, considering the size of the thing.
They dug a deep, narrow hole, dropped it in, and packed the
excavated soil back round the base. I had to admit it looked
quite impressive standing there on its own, and by the time

we'd got a few more in position we began to feel like we were getting somewhere.

We still had the problem of knocking in the pointed posts though. Donald's idea about using a stepladder had seemed a bit dodgy to me, and so it proved. We tried it for a bit but Tam complained he couldn't get his footing right, and looked as though he was about to come a cropper any moment. Finally he opted to stand on the roof of the truck to knock them in. This worked alright, but it was slow going as we had to keep moving the truck along the fence line all the time. Not very efficient really. 'The company should buy a mechanical post hammer,' I said. 'I saw one being demonstrated once. It could put a post in with a few hits.'

'I don't like the sound of that,' said Tam.

'Why not?'

'Well, it'll put me out of work, won't it?'

'Are you a Luddite then?' I asked.

'What's one of those?'

'Someone who distrusts new inventions.'

'No.'

'Well then. You don't want to be swinging a post hammer for the rest of your life, do you?'

Tam looked at me and shrugged. 'I don't mind.'

That night in the canteen we expected to see only sausages on the menu again, but instead it was steak and kidney pie. We carefully avoided conversations about the quality and quantity of the food, and instead talked about the prospect of finding a decent pub nearby.

'I think we ought to go out about seven o'clock,' said Tam. 'We should have found one by quarter past.'

'Either that, or we could go straight out after tea, find one, come back and then go out again,' suggested Richie.

'And if we don't find one we won't come back until we do.'

'Wait a minute,' I interrupted. 'Don't forget they lock the gates at six. We can't take the truck.'

'You'll have to ask them to let us out,' said Tam.

'Why me?' I asked.

''Cos you're foreman, of course.'

'I'm not asking them.'

'Well I'm not fucking walking,' he snapped.

'I don't see what choice we have,' I said. 'Unless you want to ask them.'

Tam turned to Richie. 'What do you think, Rich?'

'Looks like we'll have to walk.'

'For fuck sake.'

Back in the caravan, with the strip light buzzing loudly, we had a look at Donald's route map. His green line ended at the factory and there was nothing else. The only pub we knew was the Queen's Head, and that was miles away beyond Upper Bowland, much too far to walk.

'We'll just have to follow the Lower Bowland road,' I said. 'See where it goes.'

'Are you changing, Rich?' asked Tam.

'Well I'm putting my cowboy boots on if we're walking,' replied Richie.

'And me.'

They got ready in about two minutes. We walked down the driveway in darkness, climbed over the gate, and started our long walk in search of a pub. The road was dark and little used. From time to time we passed small settlements and solitary houses, some with curtains drawn and lights shining inside, others unlit and apparently empty. Occasionally a car would come along, the headlights beaming between the hedgerows, dazzling us, and then passing into the darkness. Once or twice we tried sticking our thumbs out, but we knew it was a waste of time. Who would stop for three strangers in the middle of nowhere, in the dark? We kept going for well over an hour, continually disappointed as the road swung round yet another long bend to reveal nothing more promising than a road sign, a red triangle on a white background, and the words SOFT VERGES FOR TWO MILES.

'We can't do this every night,' I said. 'Not when we're working all day. It'll fucking kill us.'

'Well, we'll have to ask for a key or something won't we?' said Tam.

I liked how it was 'we' all of a sudden. Tam was probably right though. We didn't want to stay in every night. That'd drive us crazy. We'd have to think about asking Mr Hall for a key tomorrow. Or maybe the day after.

After another half-mile a dull glow appeared in the distance and to our relief we finally came upon a green, with a phone box on one side and on the other a pub.

'Thank fuck for that,' said Tam.

I thought about phoning Donald to make a progress report, but decided he could wait.

The pub was called the Mason's Arms. A large Christmas tree with fairy lights had been positioned in a half-barrel by the porch, and stuck on the door was a picture of Santa Claus, smiling and ringing a handbell. The pub, however, was empty. When we entered, the publican was perched on a high stool at the end of the counter, assembling a model aeroplane. He looked surprised to see us.

'You're early,' he said, by way of greeting. 'Most people don't pop in till ten o'clock.'

'Oh well,' I said. 'Bit of extra trade for you.'

'Pint apiece, is it, lads?'

'Alright then.'

'In tankards?'

'Oh, er, no, thanks.'

'Most people ask for tankards.'

'No, no. Straight glasses. Thanks.'

'Right you are.'

I wondered if other people in other pubs throughout the land were having the same conversation. Tam and Richie had already made for a table at the far side of the room, so it looked like I was buying the first round.

As I joined them they looked glum.

'This is shite,' Tam muttered. 'There's no one here.'

'Maybe there'll be some more in later,' I said.

'Maybe.'

'Beer's piss-weak too,' remarked Richie.

So we sat at our chosen table, and waited for the evening to pass. After about half an hour the publican disappeared into a room behind the bar, leaving us completely alone. When he returned he had a mug of tea in his hand.

'For fuck sake,' said Tam quietly. 'You'd never catch Jock drinking tea when he's on duty.'

It was not until well after ten that the first locals appeared and sat around the bar on what were obviously their usual stools. The publican put away his aeroplane and moved into position behind the counter, which allowed him to take part in the various discussions the regulars were having. As one or two more people turned up in the pub a background drone developed, so that we no longer had to lower our voices to speak to each other.

'Have you noticed there are no women at the Hall Brothers' place?' I said.

'I know,' said Richie. 'Not even in the canteen.'

'Fucking none here either,' observed Tam.

Last orders meant last orders in the Mason's Arms, so we found ourselves back on the road just after eleven fifteen. The walk to the factory seemed to take much longer than the outward journey, and the weather had turned colder. By the time the gateway came into sight, the warming effect of the beer had completely worn off. As we came up the drive we saw that the loading bay was brightly lit by floodlamps. Several vans were lined up with their engines running, and the noise was augmented by the rumbling of their refrigerator units. Some of the men stopped what they were doing and looked across at us as we approached.

'What are they staring at?' said Tam.

'Nothing,' I said. 'Pay no attention to them.'

'Look,' said Richie. 'We've been burgled.'

That's what it looked like anyway. The caravan door had been thrown open and the strip light switched on. Then David

Hall appeared in the doorway, holding a dustpan and brush.

'Where have you been?' he demanded.

'To the pub,' I said.

'Haven't you got enough to do here?'

'Not really.'

'You surprise me. Who's going to wash your socks?'

'Pardon?'

'Those don't look like hands that do dishes.'

'Oh,' I said. 'No, 'spose not.'

He unblocked the door and allowed us to go inside. I couldn't tell if he'd been searching the caravan or just tidying up. Either way I wasn't sure what to say next. Maybe he was merely stamping his authority over us, but it struck me at that moment that the Hall Brothers had some very funny ideas about what was and what wasn't important. We all sat down on our respective beds as he gazed at us from the doorstep, slowly shaking his head.

'I don't know why you can't just stay home at nights,' he said at last.

'We didn't go very far,' I replied.

'Didn't say you did.'

A bell rang from somewhere inside the factory. David Hall looked at his watch, grunted and stalked off into the darkness.

'For fuck sake,' said Richie, after he'd gone. 'He's worse than my mother.'

We had a quick look round the caravan to try and see what he'd been doing, but really we were all too tired to come to any sensible conclusion.

'Who cares?' said Tam, crashing out on his bed. 'I'm going to sleep.'

This was easier said than done. The combined din of the refrigerator vans and the operations in the loading bay continued late into the night. Bells rang. Other vehicles came and went, and heavy doors were slammed shut as unknown voices gave instructions. It wasn't until after three o'clock that the last of the vans departed.

'Are you still awake?' said Tam.

'No,' replied Richie.

'Have you noticed we never see those guys from the factory going home?'

'That fucker probably doesn't let them.'

'No . . . ha. Night then.'

'Night.'

The following morning, having breakfasted on sausages, we continued work on the new fence. After a couple of hours we noticed a large party approaching from the direction of the factory. It was the men from the canteen, but instead of their white butchers' coats they were all wearing blue overalls. David Hall accompanied them.

'Got a fag, Rich?' said Tam.

Richie produced a pack of cigarettes from his shirt pocket and fished in his jeans for a light. Then they lit up and stood close together smoking. This was their excuse to stop work and watch what was going on, but I didn't mind because we'd all been working quite hard during the morning. Judging by the excited chatter we could hear anyone would have thought the men were all going on a picnic or something, but when they got to the first Hall Bros. fence we saw why they'd come out. Directed by David Hall they began dismantling the fence quickly and efficiently, taking away the old posts and wire. The make-shift demolition squad made short work of the first fence and moved on to the next one. As they laboured David Hall acted as overseer, occasionally glancing in our direction. This was enough to keep Tam and Richie motivated all day, and by the evening the first line of posts was in position. Meanwhile, all the old fences had been removed by the Hall Brothers' men, leaving us a clear site to work on. As dusk approached they headed back towards the factory, and we returned to the caravan.

'Fucking steak and kidney fucking pie again I expect,' said Tam as we lay resting on our bunks.

'Well I think their pie's quite tasty actually,' I replied.

'We still don't want it every night, do we?'

'Suppose not.'

Richie had a suggestion. 'Why doesn't one of us go out tomorrow and buy some different food of our own?'

I looked at Tam. 'What do you think of that idea?'

'Ant got any money.'

'What, nothing?'

'Nope.'

'How much have you got, Rich?'

'About a fiver.'

'Non-starter then, isn't it?'

'Yep.'

This meant, of course, that I was going to have to start

pestering Donald for some wages. Otherwise I'd end up lending Tam and Richie money, and I didn't want to go through all that again. For the time being it looked like the canteen or nothing. And we couldn't complain really. The food was good and there was plenty of tea. A little later we were sitting at our usual table when we received another visit from David Hall.

'Finished?' he said.

'Yes, thanks,' I replied.

'Want some more?'

'Er . . . no. Thanks anyway.'

'You'll be taking an early bath then, will you?'

'Well, we'll probably have a stroll down the pub later,' I said. 'Got a phone call to make.'

'And you'll be straight back?'

'Bit later, yeah.'

'I see.' He thrust his hand into his pocket and produced a bunch of silver tags indented with the words HALL BROS. 'Fix these to the fence when it's complete, can you?'

He placed them on the table in front of me.

'Actually,' I said, 'we don't normally put things like that on our fences. Normally.'

'We'd prefer it if you did,' he said.

I glanced at Tam and Richie. They were both looking with interest into their mugs of tea.

'OK, then,' I said, putting the tags in my pocket.

After David Hall had gone, Tam said, 'You didn't ask about a key.'

'No,' I said. 'Forgot.'

As we sat silently draining our mugs, Bryan Hall emptied a

pan of water over the griddle, so that it steamed and hissed. Then he began scrubbing, and paused only to glance at us when we got up to leave.

The walk to the pub wasn't so bad that night, now we knew how many bends there were to go round. It was still a long way though, and I resolved to ask John Hall for a key the following day. When we finally got to the Mason's Arms, Tam and Richie went and got the drinks in while I gave Donald a ring.

'How's it going?' he began.

'OK,' I replied. 'We've got the posts in for the first section, and we'll get the wires on tomorrow.'

'Good. Then you can connect the electricity.'

'Well, we were going to leave that until all the fences were up.'

'You're supposed to be connecting it up as you go along, section by section.'

This was news to me.

'Does it make any difference?' I asked.

'I'm afraid so,' said Donald. 'Sounds to me as if you're putting it off.'

'Not really.'

'We want to keep Mr Hall happy, don't we?'

'Spose.'

'So get it connected section by section please.'

'OK.'

'By the way,' he continued, 'your uniforms are now ready. I'll see to it that they're delivered in due course.'

'Oh . . . right. Er, any chance of some wages?'

'What for?'

'Well, we need money for food and things.'

'It was arranged with Mr Hall that you would be allowed use of his canteen three times a day.'

'I know.'

'Therefore you don't need any money.'

'But we only ever get pies and sausages.'

There was a pause.

'Don't you like Mr Hall's sausages then?'

'Yes, but . . .' At this moment the pips started going. 'That's my last coin.'

'Alright,' said Donald. 'Keep in touch.'

With that the phone went dead. I took a deep breath, crossed the green to the Mason's Arms, and went inside. Behind the bar the publican was busy applying paint to the wingtips of his plane. He gave me a bit of a welcome and said that my 'pals' had already got me a beer. Tam and Richie were sitting at the same table as the night before, in the same chairs. When I sat down they told me quietly that the landlord had been asking all sorts of questions about fencing.

'What sort of questions?' I asked.

'The usual ones,' said Tam. 'Why do they ask questions all the time?'

'Maybe he's interested,' I suggested.

'I don't go round asking people about their jobs do I?'

'No.'

'All I want is a fucking pint.'

'That's all you're getting. Donald says we can't have any wages.'

I looked at Tam and Richie's faces and wondered if Donald realized the consequences of his actions. By not sending any wages he was more or less pulling the plug on those two. I knew from my time with them that they could only work in the day if they had beer to look forward to at night. Donald didn't seem to understand this, and as usual it was me who would have to keep them going. It was me who would have to sub them until he decided to pay us. And, of course, it would be me who had to deal with the Hall Brothers.

In the event, our next encounter with them wasn't until the following afternoon when we'd got most of the wires fixed on and tightened. Richie suddenly spotted John Hall approaching from the direction of the factory and we all doubly busied ourselves with our respective tasks.

'He won't find anything wrong with this,' said Tam. 'It's dead straight.'

Mr Hall seemed to be in expansive mood.

'Yes, this'll do it,' he said, as he joined us. 'This is what will keep them under control.' He stood looking through the wires at the adjoining land, his hands thrust deep in the pockets of his white coat.

'We committed no end of good deeds!' he declared. 'Yet still we lost the school dinners! Always the authorities laying down some new requirement, one thing after another! This time it seems we must provide more living space. Very well! If that's the way they want it, we'll go on building fences for ever if necessary! We'll build pens and compounds and enclosures! And we'll make sure we never lose them again!'

While Mr Hall was speaking Tam, Richie and I stood awkwardly nearby. I wasn't sure if he was addressing us or just making some general point. Obviously the school dinners meant more to him than we'd realized. After a few moments in deep thought he glanced at us and then began to examine the fence again.

'You'll be connecting the electricity next, I gather.'

'Yes,' I said. 'Should be doing that tomorrow.'

'That's good. The sooner it's done the better.' Mr Hall gave his new fence another look, and then returned the way he'd come.

'I'll be glad when we get back on a normal job,' said Tam.

I couldn't agree more, but we had to get this one done first, so as soon as John Hall had gone I got Tam and Richie going again fixing the barbed wire at the top of the fence. This turned out to be a real struggle. It was hard enough working with barb at normal height, but we were having to do it at the top of a seven-foot fence, and there were four strands as well. We got in all sorts of tangles and it was dusk before we finally got the last wire on. Exhausted, we trudged back towards the factory yard in the mounting gloom, with nothing to look forward to more than steak and kidney pie. As we approached the caravan we noticed that the light was on.

'For fuck sake,' I said. 'Now what?'

We opened the door and looked inside. Morag Paterson was sitting on the end of Tam's bed.

16

'Morag, what are you doing here?' said Tam, as she rose to greet us.

'Just paying you a visit,' she replied. 'See how my boys are keeping.'

She was wearing some kind of uniform. It consisted of little more than a simple overall, but the design was such that all the fastenings were concealed. Around the waist she wore a broad belt that served no obvious purpose other than to emphasize the cut of the fabric, which lay more or less perfectly over every contour of her body.

The three of us stood there gawping at her for a few moments before Tam managed to say, 'Well, it's great to see you. Your outfit looks very . . . tight.'

She smiled.

'It just needed a tuck here and a tuck there. You know. Lift and separate.'

'Er . . . like a cup of tea or something?' I asked.

'I'd better give you these first.' A box had been placed on the other bunk, and under the glare of the strip light Morag now began to remove the packaging.

'I've brought your new uniforms,' she said. 'Special delivery.'

'What, from the company?' said Tam.

'Of course.'

'I didn't know you'd joined.'

'Oh, Donald's recruiting all the time. I'm his latest. We've been working very closely together.'

'Have you?'

'Very closely indeed.'

The uniforms had been neatly pressed and folded. They were only overalls really, but they all bore an emblem depicting a sort of half-open portcullis.

'What's this?' I asked.

'The new company insignia,' replied Morag.

'And when are we supposed to wear these?'

'All the time.'

'Not at night, though, surely?'

'While you're here you represent the company. Therefore you should wear your uniform at all times.'

'Therefore?'

'Correct. Now I must go and pay my respects to Mr Hall. After all, I am his guest.'

Morag ran a hand through her hair and slipped out of the caravan into the night. As soon as she'd gone Tam clapped his hands. 'Waap!' he cried. 'You two'll have to sleep in the truck tonight! Ya haa!'

'We're still going to the pub though, aren't we?' said Richie.

'Fucking right!' said Tam, looking at me. 'Alright for a sub?'

'OK,' I said.

'Right,' he said. 'We'll get changed now and as soon as she comes back we can go out.'

Morag's arrival had certainly revived Tam's spirits. I hadn't seen him so enthusiastic for quite a while, although it struck me that he was taking certain things for granted. Very soon kettles were being boiled and hair was being washed as we all 'got ready'. Then we sat down and waited for Morag to come back.

'We forgot to go to the canteen,' I said, after a while. 'It'll be closed now.'

'That's alright,' said Tam. 'We'll get something later.'

'We're going to look like cunts in those outfits,' remarked Richie.

'Well, Morag looked good in hers.'

'She'd look good in anything,' said Tam. 'What's keeping her anyway?'

An hour had passed since Morag left us, which seemed a bit of a long time.

'We've got to see Mr Hall about a key,' I said. 'Why don't we go now?'

'Go on then,' said Tam.

'All of us,' I said.

'Why?'

''Cos I'm not going on my own.'

Tam tutted. 'C'mon then.'

When we got round to the offices they were all in darkness, but there was the usual level of activity in the factory, so we went in through the side door. Once inside we could hear the sound of refrigeration equipment rumbling, and sausage machines doing their work. There were men here and there attending to various production processes. In the centre of the factory floor was a small square office with a frosted glass panel in the door, bearing the words FOREMAN. Behind it we could see two white shapes beneath a single light-bulb. I knocked and one of the shapes came and opened the door. It was David Hall.

'Aha, the truants return,' he said, holding the door open for us to enter.

Inside, John Hall was sitting behind a large desk, examining some papers. Without looking up, he indicated three wooden chairs in front of him. We sat down, side by side, as David Hall went out and closed the door.

'Now then,' said John Hall. 'What can I do for you?'

'Well,' I said. 'We were wondering if we could have a key for the front gate.'

'A key?'

'Yes.'

'Why's that?'

'So we can go out at nights.'

'Nothing was said about any key.'

'No . . . but we wondered if we could have one anyway, that's all.'

Mr Hall looked up. 'Nothing was said about any key,' he repeated. 'You should try studying the small print. There's definitely nothing about any key. Not one word. And if you don't mind my saying so you seem to be treating this place as some sort of holiday camp where you can do what you please. You're always going off somewhere or other. You remind me of herds of wildebeest constantly roaming round in search of water. It's not as though we haven't done our best to accommodate you. Bent over backwards we have, yet all you do is complain about our pies and sausages. You're never satisfied with what's laid on. It so happens that my brother Bryan prepared something special this evening by way of a change. You'd have known that if you'd had the courtesy to turn up in the canteen at the appointed hour. Now you've gone and upset him and he won't get over it for days. Taken it most personally he has. And you walk in here and ask for a key. Bit of a liberty I'd call it.'

'So we can't have one then?' I asked.

'I'm afraid not,' replied Mr Hall.

A moment passed.

'Where's Morag?' said Tam.

'The girl? She's gone.'

'Gone?'

'Oh yes. We couldn't allow a woman like that to remain on the premises for very long. The men would have found it too disturbing.'

'But she can't have gone.'

'Come, come,' said Mr Hall. 'Do you think the whole world revolves around your every whim and fancy?'

'No.'

'Well, then. We all have our disappointments, you know. How do you think I feel about losing the school dinners?'

'That's different.'

'No, it isn't different. It's the same. Disappointment is disappointment. You should know all about that. You've left a trail of very disappointed people behind you.'

Mr Hall sat silently regarding us across his desk. The only sound was the endless churning of the sausage machines, somewhere in the depths of the factory. My chair had begun to feel very uncomfortable.

'What people?' I asked.

'Well,' he said. 'Let's start with Mr McCrindle.'

*

in memory of Shaun Scapens